PRAISE FOR

PENNY WARNER

Macavity, Anthony, and Agatha Award Winner

"Connor Westphal is one enjoyable heroine. She is independent; has an attitude that makes dull people cringe; and is deaf. Penny Warner manages to slip in quite an education for the hearing public, and to make us laugh in the process.... *Blind Side* is one raucous mystery, and Warner is a helluva writer."

—*Midwest Book Review*

"A sprightly, full-fledged heroine, small-town conniptions, frequent humor, and clever plotting makes [*Blind Side*] a strongly recommended purchase for most collections."

—*Library Journal*

"Warner leads readers on a merry chase full of red herrings (and frogs) before we get to whodunit. Connor's deafness is matter-of-factly handled; indeed, her lip-reading ability makes her eavesdropping easier. This is an entertaining puzzle in a smartly wrapped package."

—*Contra Costa Times*

"Penny Warner's feisty deaf heroine, always on the track of a catchy headline, will foil all intentions of a siesta.... Dan and Connor have a warm carefree connection; the innuendos and banter are delicious. Warner has a gift for dialogue.... Each of the books in the series illustrates the day-to-day circumstance of deafness.... There is nothing in recreational mystery reading with a deaf protagonist like this."

—*Silent News*

"Warner's fifth mystery...mingles mayhem at the annual Jumping Frog Jubilee with large doses of humor, a dash of romance, and a soupçon of murder.... Warner's sensitive handling of disabilities adds a nice dimension to the series.... The characters are appealing and Connor's grit and pluck make her an easy heroine to root for."

—*BookBrowser*

SILENCE IS GOLDEN

A Connor Westphal Mystery

Penny Warner

PERSEVERANCE PRESS / JOHN DANIEL & COMPANY
PALO ALTO / MCKINLEYVILLE, CA · 2003

This is a work of fiction. Characters, places, and events are the product of the author's imagination or are used fictitiously. Any resemblance to real people, companies, institutions, organizations, or incidents is entirely coincidental.

A PERSEVERANCE PRESS BOOK
Published by John Daniel & Company
A division of Daniel & Daniel, Publishers, Inc.
Post Office Box 2790
McKinleyville, CA 95519
www.danielpublishing.com/perseverance

BOOK DESIGN: Eric Larson, Studio E Books, Santa Barbara
www.studio-e-books.com

Cover photo hand-tinted by Linda B. Lewis

10 9 8 7 6 5 4 3 2 1

LIBRARY OF CONGRESS CATALOGING-IN-PUBLICATION DATA
Warner, Penny.
  Silence is golden : a Connor Westphal mystery / by Penny Warner.
    p. cm.
  ISBN 1-880284-66-9 (alk. paper)
  1. Westphal, Connor (Fictitious character)—Fiction. 2. Women journalists—Fiction.
3. Deaf women—Fiction. 4. Prospecting—Fiction. I. Title.
  PS3573.A7659S57 2003
  813'.54—dc21
                2002156709

To Tom, Matthew, and Rebecca

ACKNOWLEDGMENTS

Thanks to everyone who helped with the manuscript in
some form or another: Colleen Casey, Rena Leith, Ann Parker,
Constance Pike, Diana Todd, the folks at the
Mother Lode Café, and the Teabuds.
And a special thanks to my editor, Meredith Phillips.

Such was life in the Golden State:
Gold dusted all we drank and ate,
And I was one of the children told
We all must eat our peck of gold.

—Robert Frost

SILENCE IS GOLDEN

☞ Chapter 1.

"COLD!"

Seventy-two-year-old Sluice Jackson, Flat Skunk's oldest living prospector, didn't look cold, dressed in his usual denim overalls, plaid flannel shirt, and old miner's cap, all dusted in the red dirt of the Gold Country. With ribbons of sweat curling down his weathered face, he looked downright blistering hot.

No wonder. Yesterday Flat Skunk had set a new heat record for August at 112 degrees. It hadn't been that hot around here since 1908.

That's why Dan Smith and I were sitting on a bench in front of the *Eureka!* newspaper building instead of sweltering inside with no air-conditioning. At least this way we could catch a breeze every now and then from the tourists passing by.

Besides, there was no pressing need to be at my computer. It had been a slow news day in Flat Skunk—a slow news month, for that matter. My last headline had read HEAT WAVE SCORCHES SKUNK, followed by a bunch of clichéd reactions from the locals. In essence, everyone agreed that this hot spell stank. Literally. You could smell the skunk weed this time of year.

As for Dan, ex-New York cop turned private investigator, the heat had doubled his workload. People get crabby when it's over a hundred around here. At the moment, Dan was taking a break between jealous-lover stakeouts and missing-persons reports, sipping on a Sierra Nevada Pale Ale wrapped in a paper bag.

And then there was the heat between the two of us, which upped my personal thermometer.

"*Cold!*" Sluice hunched over and repeated the word in my face. His breath smelled of alcohol and peanuts—not a good combination on a hot day. I pulled back in an attempt to get a fresh breath of air.

"What's the matter, Sluice? You sick or something?" Maybe he had a fever that was giving him a chill.

Or maybe I had misread his lips. Wouldn't be the first time, especially with Sluice, who tended to mumble beneath that foot-long, bug-trapping gray beard.

Out of the corner of my eye, I saw Dan laugh. "What?" I snapped, frowning at both of them.

"*Gold,*" Dan said, over-enunciating the word. Then he made the sign for "gold," which also doubles as the sign for "California." "He's saying 'gold,' Connor. Not 'cold.'" He tightened his fists and shivered them, indicating the sign for "cold."

I looked back at Sluice. He held up a miner's poke—a small, well-worn leather sack tied with drawstrings. Sluice glanced suspiciously up and down the wooden plank sidewalk, checking for Russian spies, neo-Nazis, New York muggers, or whatever loomed in that muddled head of his. When he was sure the coast was clear, he pulled open the drawstring bag and stuck his stout, cracked fingers inside, fumbling around for something.

He withdrew two fingers and held them up in the shape of a V. Between the V was a gold nugget the size of a tooth.

I glanced at his snaggle-toothed grin to make sure he hadn't lost one of his own. There were only a few teeth left in that old head of his, and he couldn't afford to lose another. Those he had were crowned with gold.

"Where'd you get that, Sluice?" Dan asked, turning so I could read his lips while he talked. He was thoughtful that way. Not every hearing person was.

Sluice quickly dropped the nugget back in the pouch, then stuffed the pouch deep into his ragged overall pocket and buttoned it closed. I half expected him to pull out a padlock. Instead he glanced up and down Main Street again, leaned in, and said, "Over yonder, up Buzzard Hill." He nodded his head in the direction of the golden foothills just beyond Flat Skunk.

"You mean Chester Orland's property?" Dan asked.

Chester Orland owned several hundred acres in Calaveras County, inherited from his father, Redding Orland, his grandfather, Corning Orland, and his great-grandfather, Orville Orland. Orville had struck it rich back in the late 1850s, but after the initial strike, the land hadn't produced much gold ore. Folks said Chester Orland was planning to turn the area into a giant water-themed amusement park modeled on the old wooden flumes that carried logs and water down from the mountains. He was going to call it "Glory Hole Rapids." Even had the signs made up before the plan fell through. Cool idea, though, especially on a sizzling day like today.

"Chester know about it?" I asked.

Sluice frowned defensively. "I got permission. Chesty said I could prospect up there all I wanted. He reckons there's still gold on his prop'ty and if I found anythin' I could keep it. Long as I tol' him."

While Sluice rambled on with details of discovering the nugget, my mind drifted. Was there really more gold in them thar hills? There had always been traces, flakes, what-have-you, but there hadn't been a real find since the Forty-niners cleaned out the place. Back then the Mother Lode was a source of potential wealth to would-be miners with gold fever. Just the whisper of the word "gold" sent shivers up and down spines, up and down the Gold Chain. Thousands of men and a handful of women had rushed to California to make a fortune from the glittering rivers and sparkling mines.

But when the gold ran out, the miners moved on to the next strike. Today the Gold Country offers wannabe prospectors a few flakes, mostly "discovered" in salted mines and sluices. Descendants of the old Forty-niners now find their gold in tourists' pockets, leading unsuspecting amateurs on "authentic" gold-panning tours.

"And there's more," Sluice continued, interrupting my ruminations on local history. "Chesty says anyone who finds a real vein gits to share profits fity-fity. And he's planning to start selling int'rest in the property, too, so's he can pay for gold recovery 'quipment."

"Well, congratulations, Sluice," I said patiently. "You might end up a rich man after all those years of digging up dirt." That reminded me of what I do for a living, dig up dirt for the *Eureka!*. But I had a feeling Sluice had a better chance of hitting pay dirt than I ever did.

Sluice grinned again. The gold crowns glistened in his saliva. He mumbled something I couldn't make out and trotted on down the rickety wooden sidewalk toward the center of town. It looked like he was headed for Phil Meredith's office, the town assayer. Of course, that was a part-time job for Phil, since gold discoveries were about as common as dot-com successes these days. Phil also served as a jeweler, appraiser, rock hound, and amateur historian. No one in this town seemed to work at only one job—except me.

Dan watched Sluice go, then turned to face me so I could

read his lips. "Sounds like a story, Connor. You going to do a little digging yourself?"

"What?" I said. "You can't be serious. I mean, I love Sluice, but he's missing a few nuggets himself, after sixty-some years of drinking liquid gold in the form of homemade moonshine."

Dan shrugged. "That was a pretty big nugget."

"Oh, no. Don't tell me that's gold fever burning in those dark eyes of yours? And I thought it was lust." I wiped the beads of sweat from my forehead with the back of my hand, trying to make the gesture look sexy, like Dorothy Lamour in that old volcano movie. I don't think it turned him on as much as I'd hoped.

But before I could start flirting in earnest, someone tapped me on the shoulder, startling me. I whirled around to face Jeremiah Mercer, my twenty-six-year-old assistant at the newspaper and Sheriff Elvis Mercer's son. Miah runs his own surf shop in my building, even though there's no surf anywhere near the Gold Country. His shop also offers underground comic books, trendy trading cards, weird candy, sassy bumper stickers, and other contraband for kids. He's a great source for my favorite Gold Key comics, especially *Little Lulu*.

"Did you hear?" Miah signed fluently, which at this moment consisted of pointing to his ear and raising his eyebrows. He'd been taking classes at the community college and had quickly become skilled in American Sign Language.

"What?" I struck my palm with an index finger.

"Gold found!" Miah continued, using ASL syntax. "Buzzard Hill. Sluice tell me."

"Really?" I signed, pushing my index finger from my chin. "I thought he wanted to keep it a secret." I signed and said the words aloud so Dan would be included in the conversation. Although Dan knows some signs, he isn't nearly as fluent as Miah. His body Braille is excellent, however.

"Sounds like tomorrow's headline," Miah signed and said simultaneously. "Beats the weather bulletins, anyway."

"We can't print anything until it's confirmed," I said. "And you know Sluice. He's not always the most...reliable source. Remember those aliens he was sure he saw over in Lousy Ravine? Turned out to be cows dressed up for Halloween—"

Something caught my attention in the distance beyond Miah. Two men had just burst out of the Nugget Café and were running toward us. I jumped up, wondering if something had happened at Mama Cody's diner. A fire? No smoke. A heart attack? I wouldn't be surprised, with Mama Cody's high-cholesterol food. A real story for the *Eureka!*?

Wolf Quick, former jewelry store owner, now ex-con, and Jake Passage, former construction worker, future ex-con, slowed down as they approached us. Instead of stopping, as expected, they tried to hurry around me. I blocked their path with both hands up.

"Whoa, guys! What's up?" I said. "Something happen at the Nugget?"

Jake glanced at Wolf, who gave him a look that clearly read, "Keep your mouth shut." Jake was not the brightest bulb in the socket, but Wolf was as slick as the sweat on my forehead. I'd never trusted him, even before he'd been arrested for jewelry fraud.

"N-no...nothing," Jake stammered as he warily moved around me, following Wolf. They took a few more steps, looked back in my direction, then froze in their tracks. I followed their gaze back to the Nugget. A herd of about twenty café patrons was stampeding out of the restaurant, all heading our way.

Jake and Wolf took off.

"What is it?" I shouted, as a few townspeople ran past us. "What's going on?"

No one stopped to answer my questions, so Dan grabbed the first arm he could reach, pulling Jilda Renfrew to a sudden halt. The part-time Nugget waitress/manicurist/massage therapist gave Dan a look that would peel the polish off inch-long nails.

"Let go!" she said. Dan released her.

"What's going on, Jilda?" Dan demanded. "Did something happen at the Nugget? Is someone hurt?"

"Gosh, no!" Jilda said. "Just me, thanks to you grabbing my arm." She rubbed the spot where Dan had grabbed her. There wasn't a mark anywhere.

"What is it then, Jilda?" I asked.

"Haven't you heard?" Jilda's face lit up. The pain in her arm had apparently vanished.

"I haven't heard anything for over thirty years," I said sarcastically, referring to my bout with meningitis at the age of two. The illness had left me permanently deaf. She didn't appear to get it.

"Sluice Jackson found *gold*!"

So much for Sluice's attempt to keep his discovery secret.

———•———

It turned out that everyone from the Nugget Café was headed for Wolf's new gold mining store to buy supplies. Yelling the word "gold" in a town full of wannabe miners is like yelling "chocolate" at a PMS support group. This mini-stampede turned out to be the tip of the miner's pick. Once word spread—with the help of the *Eureka!* of course—strike-hungry tourists within an eight-hour drive had bought up all the supplies, booked all the bed-and-breakfasts, and overrun our "gold chain" of charming antique towns. The crowds would be good for Flat Skunk's economy, but bad for those of us who just wanted to make our gold the old-fashioned way—by hard work and hard copy.

Yep, thanks to Sluice Jackson's find, things wouldn't be the same in the Mother Lode for some time. Not after Phil Meredith, the assayer, appraised that gold nugget and discovered its true worth.

And especially not after Sheriff Mercer found out who it really belonged to.

☞ CHAPTER II.

I LOOKED AT DAN. He looked at me.

A whole conversation passed silently between us, and we headed briskly for the assayer's office. At least we kept our dignity and didn't flat-out run like the rest of the crowd. I'd never seen anything like it. It was something out of a B horror movie: *The Town That Went Berserk for No Apparent Reason Except the Mention of the Word 'Gold.'*

Maybe if we'd run we'd have been able to see what the commotion was all about at the assayer's front counter. But by the time we arrived, the small room was full of gold diggers pushing and shoving to see Phil Meredith do his magic.

Someone jostled me from behind and I whirled around to jostle him back. It was Sheriff Mercer. He said something like, "Stand back! Stand back!" Of course, it could have been "Dan Black" or "tan pack." His lips were distorted by his shouting. But considering the context, I'm pretty sure that's what he was commanding. I watched him try to swim upstream through the crowd. The jostling he received caused his hearing aid to pop out and dangle at the side of his ear.

I lost sight of the sheriff for a few minutes, after being knocked, pushed, and shuffled about by the bobbing and weaving swarm. I finally spotted him climbing up onto the assayer's front counter. Breathing hard, he pulled himself to standing, as if he'd just climbed Buzzard Hill, tucked in his hearing aid, and gazed over the sea of gold-hungry pirates. He held his hands up in an attempt to calm the turbulence, but the surf was up.

"Simmer down, folks. Simmer down!" I think the sheriff said. It was difficult reading his lips with all those bobbing heads in the way. Sheriff Mercer flapped his arms and kept shouting, and eventually the shuffling slowed. All eyes were on the sheriff, even as the door kept opening and closing. More bodies shoved their way in, carrying picks, pans, and prospecting gear, no doubt freshly purchased from Wolf Quick's new shop a few doors down.

I noticed one couple in particular, only because the man and woman had dressed alike. Both wore cargo pants, nearly every inch covered with some sort of pocket, and matching T-shirts printed with the words ARCHEOLOGISTS JUST PLAIN DIG IT. The only difference—hers was printed in rhinestones.

Tired of being pushed around and anxious to see what Sheriff Mercer had to say, I tunneled my way to the middle of the crowd until I could read his lips. I caught him in mid-sentence.

"...Jackson is here to find out the value of the gold nugget he found on Chester Orland's property. I'm sure Phil will have that information in a few minutes. In the meantime, I need to remind you that the Orland property is privately owned and no one is allowed on it without permission."

Someone in front of me waved and apparently asked a question, but all I could see was the guy's back. Before I could ask someone to repeat the words, Dan came up beside me.

"What about Sluice?" Dan mouthed to me. "I wonder if he had permission?"

I shrugged and turned back to the sheriff, who was again in mid-sentence.

"…apparently Sluice did have permission from Chester Orland, although I'll be confirming, of course. In the meantime—"

Sheriff Mercer paused, staring at the back of the crowd. All eyes, including mine, turned to the open door of the shop. Chester Orland stood in the doorway. He looked like every other aging prospector in Flat Skunk, wearing dirty jeans with a leather belt, a beer logo T-shirt, and a cowboy hat. I strained to watch his lips.

"Greetings, everyone. Sorry to interrupt, Sheriff, but I heard there was some commotion here, on account of Sluice's find. Thought I'd drop by and let you all know how Sluice made his discovery. It's a pretty amazing story, right, buddy?"

I glanced at Sluice, who was hovering over Phil, who was hovering over the nugget. Sluice was watching Phil so intently, he didn't seem to notice the huge crowd gathered around him. By now everyone was gazing at Chester Orland, hanging on his every word as if he were some kind of prophet.

"What Sluice told you is true. My old buddy here had my permission to look for gold on my property, even though I didn't think there was much of a chance he'd find anything after all these years. As you know, the mines have pretty much dried up. I was working on that big old water park for the kids until it fell through. We'd even made the first dig. But this nugget Sluice found in the bulldozed piles may change all that, depending on what Phil here says, of course."

The eyes shifted to Phil, who was still hunched over the nugget, gazing at it through a jeweler's loupe. The magnifying eyepiece was attached to an elastic band that he wore around his forehead most of the time. I could see the circular dent in his skin from the constant pressure it must have applied. Phil glanced up for a second, took in the crowd around him, then returned to studying the sample, moving the nugget closer, turning it around.

"If it turns out to be authentic," Chester continued, "and worth something, I invite you all to come to the Orland property and search for more."

A roar rumbled up from the crowd, so loud even I heard it. I can hear very low and very high sounds, and while this sound may have just rumbled through the wooden floorboards, I'm pretty sure I heard it. At any rate, I sensed the natives were restless.

Chester raised his arms to calm them, then went on. "Whatever you find, I'll share with you, fifty-fifty. Seems only fair, since I own the property."

Heads nodded vigorously. And no wonder. If they each managed to find a few more nuggets the size of Sluice's, they'd have more than enough to buy a couple of boats, a new motor home, and maybe even an SUV for the wife—and girlfriend.

Chester raised his arms again and faced the crowd. "I have another offer to make…" He turned to me and continued, "and I'm hoping Ms. Westphal here will announce it publicly in her newspaper."

I raised a noncommittal eyebrow.

"I'm going to offer investment shares in the property, which will allow us to purchase the equipment we'll need to retrieve the gold. Those rotary drill rigs and air compressors and stuff are expensive—but they're the most efficient way to drill and extract the gold, and the payoff will be tenfold."

Once again the crowd cheered loudly enough for me to hear.

"So," Chester continued, "we'll wait to hear from Phil how much Sluice's nugget is worth, and then you can all decide if you want a piece of the rock, so to speak."

Everyone focused on Phil. He replaced the loupe on his forehead, swiped his wispy hair back, and stood, holding the nugget between his thumb and finger. He wiped his sweaty hand on his black T-shirt, then held the nugget up to the light bulb dangling overhead. I thought I saw it actually sparkle. Or it could have been the greed reflecting from the eyes in the room.

The crowd grew still. Sheriff Mercer remained standing on top of the counter to ensure crowd control, while Phil Meredith turned to address the eager faces. I swear, some of the guys were actually drooling.

Phil took a deep breath, still holding the nugget high in the air. "I'm going to have to do some chemical analyses to determine the proportion of gold, but as of now, it looks nearly twenty-four-carat. With gold prices today at five hundred dollars an ounce, this nugget weighing about four troy ounces, if it's truly high-grade ore we're looking at a pretty penny for Sluice here."

Although one nugget does not a discovery make, the crowd seemed to think otherwise. You've heard the expression, "the noise was deafening." I don't know what that means exactly, but for me the noise was more like "hearing." And I'd had enough sound for one day. I squeezed my way back through the thundering crowd and stepped out of the assayer's office for a breath of fresh, albeit hot, air and some peace and quiet.

As I sat down on the bench outside the assayer's office, I wondered what kind of slant I could use for tomorrow's newspaper headline. EUREKA! GOLD DISCOVERED! seemed a little overstated and ambiguous. And a story like that would bring people from all over the world, let alone the local area. All we needed were more rhinestone gold diggers, like that matching couple. While it would sell a lot of newspapers, I wasn't sure I wanted to sacrifice the serenity of the Mother Lode for sales.

Who was I kidding? Word would spread around here like a case of head lice without any help from the *Eureka!*.

"Working on a headline, aren't you?" Dan asked, sitting down beside me.

"How about something like, 'All That Glitters...' or 'Fools Discover Fool's Gold'?" I said.

"You sound skeptical. Don't you think there's more gold up there on Buzzard Hill?"

"It's only a nugget."

"Did you hear everything Phil said back there?" Dan asked.

I gave him a look.

"You know what I mean. That little ball of ore is worth some money. To Sluice, it's a fortune."

I nodded, but I couldn't help seeing a headline that read SLUICE'S FOLLY. Something wasn't right. There hadn't been a major gold discovery in these parts for decades, and all of a sudden, this?

"Maybe Chester salted the area to get people to buy into his investment proposal," I suggested. "Could be another one of his money-making schemes, like the last few he's tried over the years. Remember the Golden Hills Golf Club? That was a fiasco. Too hilly to play."

Dan nodded. "I was here when he tried to turn it into Gold Kountry Kamp Ground. Nobody came because there weren't enough sewage facilities, water, or flat campsites. Another disaster."

"Not to mention the Golden Gills Trout Farm that ended up with a bunch of floating fish, the Gold Mountain Nature Park where all the wild animals mysteriously escaped one night, and the Guaranteed Gold Mining Tours that were abandoned after that old mine caved in."

"So you think it might be another one of his money-making ventures and he's duped poor Sluice into being his stooge? You're awfully cynical these days, Connor."

"I'm just cautious, that's all. I'd hate my newspaper to be a party to his plan if it's not legit."

The door to the assayer's office swung open, and people began pouring out of the small building. After the gold dust had cleared, I ventured back inside to talk with Phil, Sluice, and the sheriff. But Chester Orland caught me before I could make my way to the counter.

"Ms. Westphal! Just the person I was looking for. How about that story? Would you like to interview me now or later?"

The arrogance. I hated being used for the power of the press. Unfortunately, it came with the job.

"I suppose…" I glanced at Sheriff Mercer, hoping he might be able to help stop the madness. But he was busy with Phil. "Uh…"

"I've got an appointment with Mike Melvin, the geologist from over in Whiskey Slide, in about an hour. He's gonna come check out the area and validate the claim. You wanna do it now?"

I looked at my watch, stalling for time. I wasn't ready with questions and wanted a little time to prepare. "How about my coming to your meeting with the geologist?" I suggested.

He shifted his weight, then said, "I better check with him on that. He might not want the press involved, and all."

Or Chester didn't want the press there, so he could give the report his own spin. "All right, come by my office after you have the geologist's report."

Chester grinned. "Sounds good. In fact, I'm thinking of putting a big old ad in your paper about selling investments. This could be a real bonanza for you, too, Westphal."

I smiled grimly. I hated the thought of selling space to a money-hungry guy like this, but then, baby needed a new pair of shoes. Baby being me. The shoes being seventy-five-dollar Doc Martens.

PENNY WARNER

"I'll see you at the *Eureka!* then," I said, glancing toward the sheriff. I wanted to catch him before he left, and his body language was showing signs of departure.

"Will do," Chester said cheerily. "Save me a half page for the ad, will you? And the cover for the story!" With that, he tapped his Stetson and headed out the door.

By the time I approached the sheriff, Sluice, and Phil, Dan had already joined the group. "So, Sheriff, what do you think of all this?" I asked him.

He rubbed his extended belly as if he were Buddha and his tummy might offer him wisdom. "Don't know. Might check the area, although this is kinda out of my league. I'll leave it to Mike Melvin, see what he has to say. Phil has tentatively assessed the value of the nugget, and I trust his skills."

Phil stuck one hand in his jeans pocket and lowered his head. A few wisps of hair dangled down and he swiped them back with his free hand. Phil had always been a shy man who didn't socialize much, and he'd become even more introverted since his wife, Rena, had left him a few months ago. Since then he'd basically lived in his office. Sheriff Mercer had tried to befriend him after Rena took off, since he'd been through something similar himself with his own wife a few years ago. But Phil hadn't pursued the sheriff's suggestions for meeting new women, and Sheriff Mercer had finally given up. I felt sorry for the guy, and wondered what had caused his wife to leave behind such a sad sack.

"What about you, C.W.?" asked the sheriff. "You going up there and snoop around for gold, too—or just dig for dirt? Too bad there's no mystery here so you'd have a reason to nose around and get into trouble."

Since when did I need a reason to get myself into trouble?

☞ CHAPTER III.

I HAD AN HOUR or so before I had to meet with Chester and
compromise my journalistic ethics. But God, those Doc Martens
were calling my name, and I was sure I'd need some new ones after digging around in the red dirt of the Sierra foothills. I had to
be there if a story turned up. Like they say, trouble follows money.
I had a feeling trouble also follows gold nuggets.

"Where are you going?" I asked Dan, as we reached the Penzance Building that housed the *Eureka!*, Miah's surf/comic shop,
and Dan's private investigation office. He didn't look like he was
heading for the outdoor staircase.

"Uh...I've got to run a few errands for this case I'm working
on...." If he'd just stolen a TV set from a storefront window, he
couldn't have looked more guilty.

I took a step back down the staircase and faced him directly.
"What case?"

He shrugged. I think he also blushed, but it's hard to tell under that salt-and-pepper beard.

"You know I can't discuss my cases."

"Who is she? I'll scratch her eyes out." I tried to look vengeful as I spoke, but the hundred-degree heat was sucking my motivation, and it only made Dan laugh. So much for trying to be a femme fatale.

"You're all talk, Connor." He grew somber.

"What do you mean by that?" I asked, puzzled by his change in demeanor.

"Nothing," he said. "I've got to go. Gotta do a background check for Sheriff Mercer."

I lifted one eyebrow. Took me years to learn to do that. I hoped it provided the message I intended: "Bullshit."

"What? It's true. Besides, it's confidential."

The eyebrow hadn't elicited the response I was hoping for. I tried the direct approach—a verbal bluff. "You're checking up on Chester Orland, aren't you."

Dan looked at the gutter. His body language was a dead giveaway.

"You're hiding something. What are you up to?" I asked.

He shifted his eyes to a nearby tree and studied it as if it were about to mutate or something. I pressed on. "Sheriff Mercer doesn't trust Chester Orland, does he?"

Dan eyeballed some peeling paint on the side of the building. His shifty gazing was making me dizzy.

"And he thinks Chester is up to something, just like I do!"

Dan finally faced me and held my shoulders. "Connor…"

"What? I'm an investigative reporter. This is the way my mind operates."

"Your mind doesn't operate, it conjures. Look, I'm just checking to make sure Chester can sell investments in this venture legally, and see that there aren't any misunderstandings about who owns what. It's routine."

"Nothing's routine with you, Dan Smith. Or with Sheriff Mercer," I countered.

"Honest—"

But I lost the rest of his words. I'd become distracted by a couple heading up the sidewalk, a little girl in tow. Their hands were flying all over the place.

They were signing!

Dan turned around to see what I was gawking at. And I was gawking. It was so unusual to see American Sign Language in Flat Skunk, especially addressed to anyone but me. There's lots of gesturing in these parts, but not much ASL. I continued to stare as they approached.

The man looked to be about thirty-five to forty, graying at the temples, well built, with slim hands and practiced fingers. I couldn't see his face as he bent over the little girl and signed, but his gestures were animated and clear. The woman looked maybe ten years younger—not a gray hair in her dark blond mass—but then Clairol can do that for a person. She had little makeup, wore a tank top and shorts appropriate for the hot weather, and was frowning at the man as he signed.

Both seemed totally focused on the little girl, who I assumed was their daughter. She was maybe five or six years old, and wore her dark blond hair in pigtails with little purple scrunchies holding them in place. Winnie-the-Pooh pranced with a honey pot on her purple T-shirt that matched her purple shorts and flip-flops. She had the woman's tan coloring and the man's long slim fingers.

I knew it was rude, but I couldn't keep myself from staring at them. Of course, deaf people who sign are used to being stared at.

"Do you want to do some gold panning first or ride the ponies?" the man signed. In American Sign Language he'd said, "First, gold panning, or pony-ride?" His eyebrows asked the question.

The little girl looked at the woman for an answer. She

relaxed her frown as she signed to the girl, "You, which prefer? Gold, pony-ride? You choose, you."

The girl grinned, revealing a gap in her smile from a missing tooth. She knew she had them both in the palm of her little signing hand. "Pony!" her hands said, bending two fingers on the top of her head. I was fascinated by her tiny expressive fingers. I hadn't learned Sign until I was in high school, and even then I had to go to a deaf camp to learn it. My parents had tried to raise me hearing, placing me in oral schools and forbidding me to sign. I'd had to be subversive to learn what I considered my native language.

The man was so focused on the little girl as he walked and signed, he nearly bumped into me. He turned to apologize, lifting his head and holding up his hands in a gesture of forgiveness.

We stared at each other for a moment. Then I signed, "Josh! Josh Littlefield!"

"Connor Westphal!" he signed back, looking as surprised as I felt.

"What are you doing here?" I signed, open-mouthed. I'd never expected to run into someone from Gallaudet University in this tiny town.

"Partly vacation, partly business," he signed. "Showing Susie some California history." He touched his daughter's shoulder proudly, then leaned over toward her. "Susie, this is my old friend from college, Connor Westphal." He spelled the letters of my name slowly, but the rest of the signs were rapid. "Can you say hello?"

Susie shyly signed, "Hi," using a small salute, then pulled back behind her mother's legs for security. Josh turned to his wife and signed, "Gail, this is Connor Westphal, from Gallaudet. Connor, this is my wife, Gail."

Gail's face had changed from expressive to blank, but she

nodded politely. I reached out to shake her hand, and she barely gave me her fingertips. "Nice to meet you," she signed by rote after letting go of my hand.

I wondered if she knew that Josh and I had been close at Gallaudet University. Very close.

I signed, "Likewise," by moving a "Y" back and forth between us, then returned my attention to Josh. I hadn't seen him in something like ten years, but it felt as if no time had passed. He still had those dark lashes, those long fingers, and that joyful smile. We instantly began catching up, on careers, families, and old friends from school. I was so engrossed in our conversation, I never thought of Dan. When I finally turned to introduce him, he was gone. I had a sudden knot of guilt in the pit of my stomach.

"Oh, dear…I wanted you to meet my friend Dan. I guess he…had to go to work or something. Sorry."

There was an awkward pause before Josh signed, "Not a problem. Some other time. We were about to take Susie for a pony ride, then maybe do some panning for gold."

"Sounds fun!" I signed to Susie. She grinned and pulled back behind her mother again. "Maybe, if you have time tonight, we could all meet for dinner?" I suggested. "Then you could meet Dan."

Josh glanced at Gail, and she forced a smile. "Sure," he signed. "You have a TTY number? I could give you a call when we're back at the B-and-B."

"Great!" I wrote down my number on the back of one of my business cards and handed it to Josh. "Where are you staying?"

"The Mark Twain Slept Here Bed-and-Breakfast, down the street."

I nodded. "I know the owner. Beau Pascal. Great guy."

From the corner of my eye I noticed Gail check her watch

and glance around, looking bored. She was no longer following our signed conversation. Susie had come out from behind her again and was grinning up at me. Her pink tongue stuck out through the gap in her teeth.

I don't know why, but the thought of having children someday has always frightened me. Maybe it's the responsibility for another human being that scares the crap out of me. Maybe it's because I'm an only child and didn't have any experience taking care of younger siblings. I never even baby-sat—no hearing parents would ever let me watch their hearing children. But whatever it was no longer seemed to matter. I suddenly wanted to take Susie home.

"How about Lola's?" I suggested, thinking Susie might enjoy the murals of the Forty-niners on the wall, if not the simple spaghetti dinner. "Great Italian food. Or the National Hotel has a nice dinner, too."

We agreed on Lola's, since they'd already been to the National.

"We better go," Gail signed to Josh. He nodded.

"See you tonight," Josh signed to me.

"Looking forward to it," I signed back. "Oh, and tell Beau to make his famous orange–cranberry muffins for you. They're to die for."

Thinking back, I really shouldn't have phrased it that way.

———◆———

Chester was late for his meeting at the newspaper, so I filled the time by fantasizing about Josh. He still looked great—lean and muscular. I tried to think back to my days at Gallaudet and remember why we'd broken up. We'd had fun together, enjoyed many of the same things. He was also majoring in journalism, but had decided to write political pieces for magazines instead of working for a newspaper. He'd had some success, too. A couple of his articles had made *The New Yorker*—a story about a deaf speechwriter for a past president called "Seeing Voices."

So what was it that caused the relationship to end? Jealousy? No, neither one of us dated anyone else while we were together. Lack of commitment? No, neither one of us had wanted to get married and settle down. What then?

Something clicked. I remembered Josh had been very active in the Deaf Community at Gallaudet, almost militant about the rights of deaf people. He'd been instrumental in getting the hearing president of Gallaudet fired and replaced by a deaf president. It had been quite a coup. He'd organized protests, effigy burnings, revolts, boycotts, even mini-riots. It had taken up a lot of his time and energy, I recalled. The way I saw it, there hadn't been a lot left for me.

When I graduated, I returned to California to write for the *San Francisco Chronicle*, while Josh stayed in Washington, D.C. to advocate for the hearing impaired. I hadn't thought a lot about him over the years, except when I noticed his byline on a national political piece.

Now I couldn't get my mind off him.

The door to my office burst open. The sudden movement startled me and I jumped. A crusty old man in jeans and a T-shirt stood in the doorway. He was covered with a patina of red dirt. Behind him were a couple of red-tinged shadows.

"Chester! You scared me!"

"I knocked. Then I remembered you can't hear nothing."

After I regained my composure, I checked my watch. "You're late. I have another appointment in fifteen minutes, so I can't give you much time—"

He entered the room, and the shadows followed. A touristy-looking couple I'd seen earlier at Phil's office stood on either side of him. Up close, I noticed them in more detail. The man was too small for his shirt, which caved in at the chest, while she was way too big for hers, revealing more skin than I wanted to see. They looked to be in their thirties, but could have been younger—the red smudges around their eyes emphasized their crow's-feet.

"Stop the presses, little lady," Chester said, grinning. When he spoke, he sprayed the air with a fine mist of spittle. He smelled of the red clay he'd been digging in. "What I got to show you is more important than any kinda meeting."

Chester gestured toward the man, who reached deep into his multi-pocketed combat pants and pulled out a shiny, smooth stone about the size of a tooth.

"I've already seen Sluice's nugget, Chester. I thought you were here to place an ad in the *Eureka!*."

"Oh, I'm here to place an ad, all right. And my offer still goes. Anyone who finds gold on my property shares it fifty-fifty. And anyone who invests gets a tenfold return. Ain't that right, Jim?"

"It's Tim," he enunciated clearly, reaching out to shake my hand. I gave him mine cautiously. "And this is my wife, Jana. We're the Josephs, up from Fresno. Lived there about twenty years. Came here to do some prospecting. Not much in the way of precious metals in Fresno, you know—"

It appeared Jim or Tim might ramble on forever, so I interrupted him before he gave me his whole life story.

"Nice to meet you," I said to him, then turned to Chester. "So…what's up, Chester? Do you want some publicity for your nugget or what—"

Chester Orland burst into laughter, then looked at the couple standing beside him. They began laughing, too.

The only one not laughing was me. I was considering calling the sheriff and having him remove three lunatics from my office when the laughter subsided.

Chester finally spoke up, using lots of spittle for emphasis. "This here ain't Sluice's nugget. The Josephs found another one!"

Just then Dan came in. He'd apparently heard the laughter coming from my usually quiet office. "What's going on in here? You okay?" he asked, after sizing up my still-grinning guests.

Before I could answer, Chester said, "These fine people here—Jim and Jana Joseph—they found another gold nugget, that's what's going on. Big as the one Sluice found—the size of a tooth." Chester slapped Jim/Tim on the back. He nearly fell over from the blow.

Dan took the nugget from Tim's hand and turned it over in his fingers. He studied it under the light from my office window, while Chester continued jabbering away at the two wannabe prospectors, telling them they were going to be rich. Then Dan picked up my phone and dialed.

"What are you doin'?" Chester said suddenly, losing his smile. The Josephs' faces grew blank.

"I'm calling Sheriff Mercer," Dan said, holding the nugget in his open palm.

"What're you doin' that for?" Chester angrily reached for the nugget. The Josephs looked downright petrified.

Dan closed his hand, wrapping his fingers tightly around the specimen. "You know why this gold nugget is the size of a tooth?" he asked Chester.

Chester, clearly puzzled, shook his head.

"Because it *is* a tooth. A solid gold tooth."

☞ CHAPTER IV.

"THAT AIN'T a tooth!" Chester Orland swiped at Dan's hand, knocking the bit of gold to the floor. He and Tim Joseph scrambled as it rolled under my desk. I knelt down and retrieved it from the other side.

"You're sure?" I asked Dan, holding the smooth sample up to the window light. It wasn't quite square, more rectangular, about a quarter of an inch thick, smooth on the sides but bumpy on one end. I took a closer look at the rough edge and found a small hole. The rest of it appeared to be solid gold.

Now that Dan had suggested it was a tooth, it really looked like a tooth. I glanced back up at the small group eyeing me and returned the object to Dan.

Sneering at Dan, Chester said, "You a dentist or sumpin? 'Cause if you ain't, you wouldn't know a tooth from a solid gold nugget. And that's what it is. Now gimme."

Chester lunged for Dan's hand, but Dan was faster.

"No, I'm not a dentist. But I am a former police officer. And I know a tooth when I see one—enamel, steel, or gold. This hole at the bottom?" Dan held up the tooth. "That's where the rest of the original tooth was. The gold had to have something to adhere to. The dentist probably filed down the bad tooth and used it as an anchor for the replacement."

I looked at Dan in amazement. Was there no end to his knowledge of human anatomy? Luckily, mine included.

"Well, while you people wait for Sheriff Mercer, I've got a paper to publish." I sat down at my desk and typed a few words on the computer, trying to decide on a headline. The problem wasn't what to say to grab the reader—just about anything having to do with gold would do the trick. But I was torn between what would make the better story following: GOLD DISCOVERED! or TOOTH FOUND! Each would bring a different type of explorer to Flat Skunk—those searching for great wealth and those searching for a good murder mystery.

After all, that tooth had to belong to someone.

Before I could get started, I felt footsteps on the hardwood floor under my feet. Swiveling around in my chair, I found Sheriff Mercer in the doorway. He'd made good time getting to my office, which amounted to walking across the street.

He nodded to each of us. "C.W. Dan. Chester, what's this all about?" He acknowledged the tourist couple with a glance but focused his attention on Chester, who pretty much demanded it.

"Sheriff Mercer. Thank God you're here. Now you can settle this thing once and for all. This here's a gold nugget, am I right or am I right?" He held the nugget/tooth out toward the sheriff.

Sheriff Mercer took the shiny object and examined it. Then he got out his glasses and looked it over a second time. Once his investigation was over, he peered at all of us from over his glasses.

"Looks like a tooth to me, Chester. Where did you find it?"

Chester's face flushed with anger. He reached for the tooth, but Sheriff Mercer made no effort to hand it over. Tim Joseph hadn't said much until this point, but now he began to speak to

Sheriff Mercer. "We found it near where that other prospector found his nugget," Tim said, then glanced at his wife for corroboration. "We heard the old guy talking about it at the café, so we hiked up there and, uh, just started digging around. It was practically lying there in the dirt, in a shallow hole." He stole another glance at Jana, who kept her frown.

"Up on the hill where the old Buzzard Mine is?" Sheriff Mercer asked.

Chester nodded. "Yep, same place as Sluice. After that bulldozer come through, we'll probably find the area loaded with gold. This can't be no tooth. Sluice's nugget weren't no tooth."

"Well, how about I have a look around up there and see if there's any more teeth lying around," Sheriff Mercer said. "That okay with you, Chesty?"

"You're welcome any time, Sheriff. In fact, the more the merrier, I say. The more gold we find, the richer I'll be. Let's git!"

Sheriff Mercer tipped his hat at me, then followed Chester Orland and the Josephs out of the office.

"You going with them?" Dan asked.

"Are you?"

He shrugged. I shrugged. Then we both headed out the door in hot pursuit. The temperature was rising right along with my curiosity.

—◦—

By the time we reached Buzzard Hill, the place was covered with vultures. Without the feathers. Weekend prospectors from eight to eighty years old were swarming all over the area, looking for a find like the one Sluice had made. They were searching for nuggets big enough to pay off the mortgage or buy a new home, no doubt. So much for my story. Who needed a newspaper in this town, when you had word of mouth?

While the sheriff cleared out the immediate area, I pulled out my reporter's notebook and tried to look official. Dan headed for the old mine, closed and abandoned for over half a century. The boarded-up entrance rebuffed his attempt to get inside, so he wandered off, probably looking for a hidden opening. The mines had lots of false entrances, dead-ends, and cave-ins, but many also offered a secret access, like a horizontal drift—a side access—if you knew how and where to look.

"C.W., what are you doing here?" Sheriff Mercer asked.

"Taking notes for my story, Sheriff. What else?"

"Well, stay out of the way, will you? I just got rid of these wannabes, and I don't want you stepping all over the—"

"What—crime scene? They found a tooth. That's all. It could have come loose and fallen out of someone's mouth years ago, or been knocked out in a fight, or been lost by a delirious dentist—"

Sheriff Mercer raised a hand to shush me. I'd thought he wasn't even listening, which was often the case, especially now that he had his hearing aid and could turn me on and off at will. He scanned the area, walked several paces back and forth, then spotted a shallow hole that looked freshly dug. He knelt down in the dirt and gently raked his fingers over the surface, like a man combing a woman's hair. After a few moments his hand stopped and his fingers began to poke into the red dirt. He scratched at the ground as if relieving an itch of Mother Earth's.

I couldn't read his lips from my angle, but I knew he was saying something—his jaw was moving up and down.

"What?" I asked, kneeling down. "What is it?"

He turned to face me. I suddenly noticed a crowd had gathered around the perimeter. Chester Orland and the Josephs stood watching intently with the other amateur prospectors. I saw Tim Joseph take his wife's hand and squeeze it gently. Jana Joseph seemed to be straining to keep the excitement from spilling out.

"Get my crime scene tape, will you? It's down in the squad car. I need you and Dan to cordon this area off. And bring my cell. I need my deputy over here."

"What's up, Sheriff?" Dan said, stepping up beside me as I rose. "Find another tooth?"

The sheriff stood and brushed the red dirt off his khaki pants. "Oh, there's another tooth, all right. But I think this one's inside a skull."

—◆—

While I dug the police tape out of the patrol car, Dan retrieved the sheriff's cell phone and used it to call Marca Clemens, the deputy, as well as Arthurlene Jackson, the Medical Examiner from Whiskey Slide. Both arrived soon after the calls, about the same time Dan and I finished putting up the tape that encircled a twenty-foot radius around the sheriff's find.

Dr. Jackson arrived in her ubiquitous white coat. She wore it like an accessory to a summer fashion ensemble, more suited to Fifth Avenue than Flat Skunk. Her skin was a dark contrast to the muted cream color of her suit. Her halo of tight curls glistened in the afternoon sun, but the rest of her looked as cool as a chocolate milkshake.

"Hello, Dr. Jackson," I said as she arrived at the cordoned area.

"Connor! Why am I not surprised?"

I smiled. We had a great relationship. She hassled me for bugging her, and I bugged her for hassling me. Someday we would be great friends. When she stopped hassling me and I stopped bugging her.

"I had nothing to do with it," I protested. She eyed me. It seemed when Dr. Jackson showed up, I was always in the wrong place at the wrong time.

"Let's have a look." She snapped on a rubber glove, pulled her lab coat tightly around her, and knelt down on one knee while the rest of us looked on. Brushing away the loose dirt, she managed to create a three-dimensional outline around the skull, which lay face up. There were three more gold teeth inside the skull under more dirt. Dr. Jackson lifted them carefully with tweezers and handed them to Sheriff Mercer, who stuck them in a small plastic bag provided by the deputy. He dropped the bag into the pocket of his khaki shirt. After a little more excavating, a vertebrum began to reveal itself.

"Sheriff, it looks like you've got yourself more than a skull," Arthurlene said, standing up.

Sheriff Mercer nodded. "Looks that way."

"Don't suppose you know whose skeleton that might be?" I asked.

Arthurlene shook her head and her curls danced in the light. "Nope, but whoever it is has been dead for a very long time."

———•———

While Arthurlene called for a forensic anthropologist to help retrieve the fragile skeleton, Sheriff Mercer cleared the entire hillside of prospectors, claiming the area to be a "possible crime scene."

The onlookers didn't leave without a lot of complaining, demanding their rights to look for gold with Chester's permission. And since I stood there with a notebook, most of them seemed to want to tell me what they thought of the whole thing. When the crowd finally dispersed, I noticed Sluice hunched near a mesquite bush, pawing at a small mound of red dirt. I hadn't seen him arrive. Apparently "crime scene" meant little to the old guy, who went on about his business as if he had every right.

"C.W., get him on outta here, will you?" Sheriff Mercer said to me. "Jeez. I don't want anybody in this area until we've cleared and checked it completely, you understand?"

I wanted to say I was not his gopher, but I knew better. If I scratched his back, maybe he'd rub my tummy and my magical headline would rise up before me. I moseyed over, trying not to look too much like the sheriff's lackey. Even though I was. Temporarily.

"Hey, Sluice, Sheriff says you're not supposed to be here," I said, approaching him from behind. "Crime scene. See the tape?"

He ignored me. I think Sluice has selective deafness. He only hears what he wants to hear.

"Sluice?" I went around to face him and squatted down, in case he was mumbling something important. He wasn't digging in the dirt as I expected. He was digging into his dirt-covered backpack, looking for God-knows-what. An old sandwich? A bottle of whiskey? Another gold nugget?

He pulled out a slim, leather-bound book and wiped off the dust with his filthy fingers. He only made it dirtier, but he seemed satisfied. Slowly he opened the cover to reveal an old tintype. A faded young couple and their baby, the man dressed in a high-collared suit and the woman wearing a ruffled shirtwaist, grimaced at the camera. The baby had on a long white dress.

"Who's that, Sluice?" I asked, caught up in the moment and completely forgetting about the sheriff's request. I knew so little about Sluice, and yet he was such a part of Flat Skunk that he was often taken for granted among the plentiful antiques of the town.

"My ma and my daddy. Mary and William Arthur Jackson. They called him Artie." Any relation to Arthurlene Jackson, I wondered. Guess not.

I reached out for the small photo album and took it from Sluice so I could examine the picture more closely. There was a hint of Sluice in the young man's face, the round Cornish nose, I thought, and the eyes, but not as rheumy. The chin was similar too, strong and bearded.

"Was that your baby sister, Sluice?" I asked, pointing to the infant in the white dress.

Sluice frowned and pulled the picture back. "That's me! As a young-un."

Whoops! Never call a man a girl by mistake. "Well, you were adorable! And your parents are a fine-looking pair."

Sluice flipped the page over to display two more pictures. They'd been crumpled and smoothed and inserted into the plastic holders years ago. I could tell by the yellowed edges. I had a feeling the photographs were stuck inside that plastic forever now.

I peeked over his shoulder and saw what appeared to be another picture of Sluice's father, standing next to a different woman who was also holding a baby. A child who looked to be five years old stood holding his father's hand. A second wife?

"Is that you again?" I pointed to the baby.

"Hell, no! That's my father, William Arthur. This here's my grandpappy, William Edward Jackson." He pointed to the man. "They called him Eddie."

I could see a strong family resemblance in the picture. I reached over to take it, but Sluice folded over the next page, revealing another picture.

"Gold," he said, tapping the middle of the picture. "Gold."

He handed the picture to me. The photo showed another man who could also have been related to Sluice, with that Cornish nose, flanked on either side by a couple of buddies, all covered with dirt, wearing hats, holding their hands up chest-high. Grinning, they held something in their hands.

Gold nuggets? I'd have to use a magnifying glass to see them better, since they were no bigger than a peanut. Sluice began tapping at the picture again, a little more insistently this time. I looked up to catch him mid-sentence.

"...knew it. Gold!"

"Did your grandfather find gold around here, Sluice?"

"That ain't my grandpappy," Sluice snapped.

I looked at him, surprised at his anger. "Sure looks like him— and you. Same eyes, nose, chin."

"That's my great-grandpappy, William Richard Jackson. They called him Jack."

"Your great-grandfather? When was this picture taken?"

"Around 1849 or '50. He was about thirty when he found them nuggets." Sluice tapped again on the photo.

The old tintype had held up well considering the amount of time that had passed. I wondered how the nuggets had fared. Gold was supposed to be nearly indestructible. In ancient times it had been a symbol for immortality. Had it given William Richard Jackson a long life?

"I can see the family resemblance. Who are the guys next to him?"

Sluice pointed to the man on the right. "That's Orville Orland, Chesty's great-grandpappy. I don't know the other guy."

I tried to focus on the objects they held in their hands. I was sure they were gold nuggets. That had to be the explanation for those silly grins.

Speaking of grins, all three men sported two or more gold teeth.

I looked back at Sluice. He was smiling and tapping his own tooth.

"Gold!"

☞ CHAPTER V.

SLUICE HAD BEEN trying to tell me something, but I had been distracted from the point. Instead of looking at the details of the snapshots, I'd been focusing on the people. And certainly one of those people pictured in the photo was important. But only when it came to the gold tooth.

I looked at him, surprised at my conclusion. "Sluice, you don't think that gold tooth they found is your great-grandfather's, do you?"

"That toof belongs to William Richard Jackson, my great-grandpappy."

"How can you be sure? It could belong to anyone. A lot of people had gold teeth back then."

"I know it's his toof they found in that dirt. And them's his bones that went with it. Jack Jackson, my great-grandpappy." He nodded vigorously and stood up.

I followed, brushing the dirt from my jeans.

"Sluice—" I protested, but he stopped me with a surprisingly sober glare from his rheumy eyes.

"I *know* it's my great-grandpappy."

"But how, Sluice, how do you know? It could be—"

"'Cause he disappeared right after he found that nugget he's holding in that picture. No one ever saw or heard from him again. Till now, that is."

I shrugged as he ambled toward Sheriff Mercer. He'd be the sheriff's problem now and a big one at that. Once Sluice gets ahold of an idea, he doesn't let go easily. That explains why he's been prospecting for over half a century, stubbornly hoping for a strike.

I followed Sluice to the cordoned site to find the crowd growing like ants at a picnic. We joined Sheriff Mercer, Deputy Clemens, Dr. Arthurlene Jackson, Chester Orland, the two Josephs who discovered the tooth, and Dan Smith, along with a new guy who looked to be about forty. He wore boot-cut jeans and a white T-shirt and cap that read USGS. United States Geological Survey. The geologist. He held a handful of dirt, letting it sift through his fingers. At one with Mother Earth.

I caught him mid-sentence. "…do some surveying and analysis before I know anything definitive."

He caught me staring and reached out a hand. "I'm Michael Melvin, USGS. You're Connor Westphal from the *Eureka!* newspaper?"

A little surprised, I nodded. How did he know?

"I heard you wanted to meet sometime for that news article about Chester's find. But I may have to postpone." He gave a wave at the condoned area as an explanation.

Awfully cooperative, I thought, for a government employee. I wasn't used to that. Talking to officials was usually like pulling teeth—painful, but rewarding, if I did it right. I must say, I had gotten good at obtaining information from hearing people. Maybe they think we deaf people aren't really listening.

"I understand," I said. "Just let me know when you're free and we'll take it from there. My readers will certainly want to know what you find."

He agreed, then returned his attention to Sheriff Mercer. "I'll get some equipment over here this afternoon. Should have some information to you by tomorrow morning."

Damn. I wanted my article for the *Eureka!* to be as complete and up-to-date as possible. My deadline was looming later today. Now I'd have to make up stuff. Just kidding. I'd never do that. Really. But I would have to make a slim story look like a giant exposé.

"It's getting late," Sheriff Mercer said. "Let's keep this area clear until Arthurlene's assistant and Mike and his team have had a chance to check it out. Chester, that's your job, you hear? No one allowed until we've removed the police line, understand?"

Chester nodded. He didn't seem terribly upset that part of his land was under investigation for an unexplained death. Maybe he thought it would bring in more looky-loos, searching for gold and buying up investments. Hell, maybe he borrowed the mysterious bones from the cemetery and buried them here just for the publicity. I wouldn't have put it past him. Anything to make a buck.

"Arthurlene, let me know what you find out on the body ASAP," Sheriff Mercer was saying. "I'll check to see if there are any missing persons over the past couple of decades. Got any idea how old this body might be?"

"I never speculate, Sheriff, you know that," Arthurlene said. Colleen Casey, her forensic anthropologist, arrived moments later and together they began the tedious task of carefully uncovering the old bones. We all watched, fascinated, as they lifted the skeleton, bone by bone, and placed it on a nearby gurney in the position they'd found it. The bones looked well preserved although delicate and brittle, as if they might collapse into dust any second. The gold teeth appeared to be in the best condition.

Out of the corner of my eye I noticed Sluice trying to get the sheriff's attention. Sheriff Mercer was ignoring him, barking out orders to the crowd to stay back, until Sluice poked his finger in Sheriff Mercer's chest.

"What is it, Sluice?" he asked impatiently. Sheriff Mercer actually had a lot of respect for the town icon. Sluice was part of the color of Flat Skunk, and he didn't give the sheriff much trouble, except for the occasional drunken but harmless tirades that sometimes scared unknowing tourists. Still, dealing with Sluice took a lot of patience, something Sheriff Mercer didn't always have.

Sluice shoved the photo in front of Sheriff Mercer's face and pointed to it.

Sheriff Mercer glanced at it and said, "Your great-granddaddy, I know, Sluice. You showed it to me before. I'm busy here. Can't you see?"

Sluice pointed again and said, "Toof!"

Sheriff Mercer frowned.

"The gold tooth," I said to him. What irony: The deaf interpreting for the incoherent.

Sheriff Mercer glanced at me. "What about it?"

"I think Sluice believes the skeleton you found is his great-grandfather, William Richard Jackson."

Sheriff Mercer's frown deepened. He was going to need a lot of Botox someday to smooth out those crevasses.

"That's impossible. Your great-granddaddy ran off back in 1850 or so. Took the gold he found and left his wife and kids, remember? If they hadn't been taken in by Orville Orland, Chester's great-granddaddy, they probably would have perished out here. This can't be him." The sheriff gave me a look that clearly questioned Sluice's sanity.

I shrugged.

"Gold toof!" Sluice said angrily, stabbing at the photograph repeatedly with his finger.

Sheriff Mercer sighed, then looked at Arthurlene, who'd been listening intently to the odd conversation. "Is that possible?" he asked her.

"I suppose," she said, "but like I said, I won't know anything until I do my examination."

The sheriff turned back to the old prospector. "Listen, Sluice, let Dr. Jackson do her work, and then we'll know more, all right? We'll find out if it's really your great-granddaddy, you hear?"

Sluice nodded, seemingly placated by Sheriff Mercer's promise. He didn't see the sheriff roll his eyes at Arthurlene. I was certain the sheriff didn't believe for a moment those bones belonged to Sluice's ancestor. And why should he? A lot of men had gold teeth back then. It could have been anyone. In fact, we might not ever find out who it was.

Then again, what if it really was Sluice's missing great-grandfather?

—◆—

"Dan, I'm meeting an old friend and his wife and kid for dinner at Lola's in about half an hour. Want to come?" We were headed back to town to wait for the geology report and Dr. Jackson's results. Good time to eat some pasta and drink a bottle of Chianti.

"Was that the family you were talking to this afternoon?" Dan asked, as we hiked down the hill from Chester's property.

"Yes, and where did you so rudely disappear to? I wanted to introduce you."

"You know, I had things to do."

"Well, I'd like you to meet them. How about it?"

Dan checked his watch. I could see excuses flying through his brain like shooting stars.

"Come on. I want you there," I pleaded.

When he couldn't come up with anything, he caved. "Yeah, all right. I'll meet you."

"Good. You'll like Josh. He's an old school friend of mine. I haven't seen him in nearly ten years."

"I'm sure I'll love him," he said. I could see the sarcasm in his face.

"And his little daughter, Susie, is adorable. I'd like to take her home with me."

Dan gave me the strangest look. I couldn't read it—or maybe I didn't want to. Although Dan and I had gotten closer over the past few months, we've never discussed kids, really. We'd never even discussed marriage. I figured Dan was still adjusting to being responsible for Cujo, the cat he'd inherited from his dead brother, Boone. At least the cat was still alive. That was a good sign of future parenting skills, wasn't it? I could say the same about my dog Casper. But then Casper didn't cry all night and spit up on me.

I derailed this train of thought before I rode it too far. Where was all this coming from?

Back in my office, I got the paper ready to go to press until it was time to meet Josh and his family at the restaurant named after Lola Montez. Lola had come to the Mother Lode as a young girl to make her fortune, not in gold metal, but with her golden throat. She sang for the lonely miners and took their money for a song. Legend had it she died poor and alone in the building where the restaurant is now housed. From rags to riches to rags again—that happened a lot back then.

Josh and Susie were waiting for me when I arrived a few minutes after six. There was no sign of Dan, and I assumed Gail was in the rest room, freshening up after their day of riding ponies and prospecting for gold with little Susie. I sat down across from Josh so I could read his signs clearly.

"It's so good to see you," I signed, and meant it. I found myself grinning like a gawky teenager. What was that about? Maybe it was just good to find someone I could relax and sign with and not have to struggle with every word.

We caught up on the day. Josh told me about the pony ride and encouraged Susie to join in the conversation, but she kept to herself, drawing a picture on the back of the kids' menu. I told him about the discovery, trying not to say too much in front of his little girl about the skeleton. At the first break in the conversation, when our rapidly flying fingers finally slowed down, I noticed Gail hadn't returned to the table.

And Dan was late.

"Where's your wife? Bathroom?" I signed, shaking a "T" for "toilet."

"She's not feeling well," Josh signed back. "It's just the two of us tonight." He gestured back and forth between Susie and himself. "What about your friend? Sorry, I forgot his name."

"Dan Smith," I spelled out. I didn't extrapolate on the "your friend." We were certainly more than that. "I don't know. He's probably working on a case that kept him late."

There was an awkward silence until the waiter came to take our order. Josh asked if I wanted to wait for Dan. I shook my head and signed, "Let's go ahead." Josh pointed to his selection and chose spaghetti from the kids' menu for Susie. I ordered aloud, pasta with a pesto Gorgonzola the restaurant is famous for, and asked for a bottle of house Chianti.

Once we'd ordered, the awkwardness returned. Finally Susie signed, "Draw pony" to Josh, her little baby finger wiggling expertly over her other palm, then the sign for "horse." Josh nodded and praised her picture. Susie beamed.

"She's really adorable," I signed. "You and your wife must be very proud of her."

"Actually, Connor, there's something I should tell you. Gail and I are divorced. And this isn't strictly a vacation. We came up here together to see a specialist for Susie. That's the real reason we're together this weekend. I thought you should know."

I was stunned, but tried not to show it. Deaf people aren't good at hiding emotions. You can easily see our feelings on our faces. Before I could say anything, Josh continued.

"It's all right. We haven't been together for some time. Susie's handling it well. She understands she still has two parents and knows we love her."

I nodded, not knowing what to say, then remembered Josh had mentioned a specialist. In the Gold Country? That was odd. Most specialists kept offices in the big cities, like Sacramento or San Francisco. Making sure that his daughter wasn't watching me, I signed, "Is something...I mean, Susie...is she all right?"

Josh smiled. "Oh, she's fine. The specialist we're seeing is Dr. Delia Thompson, a highly respected audiologist. Have you heard of her?"

"Oh, sure. She's very well known. Never met her, but I've read about her work in *Silent News* and other periodicals. She's an advocate of cochlear implants, right?"

Josh's smile faded as he nodded. "Yes, that's why we're seeing her. At my ex-wife's insistence. It seems Susie's hearing loss could be corrected with the surgery, and her deafness nearly eliminated, if she has the procedure."

"What's Dr. Thompson doing in the Gold Country? There aren't enough deaf people up here to keep her in business."

"Actually, she's retired. She's only seeing us as a special favor to Gail. Gail did an article on her for a magazine and they got to be good friends."

I thought about the controversy surrounding the cochlear implant. It certainly was a revolutionary new procedure. The simple surgery implants an auditory transmitter in the temporal bone behind the ear, which helps a deaf person electronically receive environmental sound and speech. After the surgery a microphone is attached behind the ear to receive sounds and convert them into signals for the auditory nerve. It doesn't work for all deaf people, only those with cochlear defects.

In other words, it simulates hearing, and is considered something of a miracle.

"Wow," I said. "When will she have the surgery?"

Josh frowned. "That's just it. Coming up here was Gail's idea, not mine. I don't want her to have the implant."

I sat back. "Why not? If it can really help her to hear..."

"Because...and I thought you of all people would understand this, Connor. Because I don't believe there is anything wrong with being deaf. As you know, the Deaf Community is a strong and supportive group with its own culture, beliefs, and language. I'm afraid that if Susie's hearing is restored, she wouldn't be a part of that community anymore—she'd be an outsider."

"But she could communicate equally in both the hearing and the deaf worlds. Being able to hear would open up so many new opportunities for her. How can you deny her that?"

Josh squirmed in his seat. There was something he wasn't telling me. I had a feeling I knew what it was.

"You're afraid, aren't you?" I signed.

"Afraid of what?" he signed, looking defensive, then picked up his wine.

"Of losing her. To the hearing world. Because you're deaf."

Josh's eyes filled with tears. He didn't say anything for a few minutes, just sipped his wine in an attempt to control his emotions. He set the glass down, stroked Susie's hair as she drew another picture of a pony, then nodded.

I nodded, too. I knew how he felt. Sort of, anyway. Without

having a child, I couldn't know exactly. But I understood his fear of losing someone to another group of people. My own parents had experienced it with me. They had wanted me to be hearing so badly that they sent me to hearing schools and never let me learn sign language. After I learned to sign on my own, I was still close to my parents, but I found surrogate parents in the Deaf Community, who understood me better than any hearing parents could. I loved my mom and dad, but there was no denying we were different.

"You were like this in college," I said. "A militant Deafie. You haven't changed a bit."

"I'm not militant. Just politically active. And I want my child to stay deaf. Only a deaf person could begin to understand the desire to have a deaf child. I really thought you would, too. Have you ever considered getting an implant yourself, Connor?"

I shook my head. "My parents want me to. They bring it up every now and then. But I'm comfortable the way I am. Besides, all the surgery, and having that thing in my head—no, I think it's too late for me."

"I wish Gail understood that," Josh said.

"But as a deaf person, why is Gail pushing for the cochlear implant? I realize not every deaf person thinks deafness is okay, but doesn't she feel she might lose Susie to the hearing world, too?"

"Oh, I thought you knew. Gail isn't deaf. She's hearing."

☞ CHAPTER VI.

I ALMOST CHOKED on my wine. "Your wife—ex-wife—she's hearing? But I thought you…" I didn't know how to phrase my last words. He finished my sentence for me.

"You thought I didn't like Hearies. Obviously it's not true. What bothers me are the Hearies who try to tell us Deafies what's best for us. Gail wasn't like that. She's a CODA. She grew up with deaf parents, became involved in the Deaf Community, and is an advocate for the Deaf, really. That's one of the reasons why I was attracted to her."

CODAs, Children of Deaf Adults, are almost always accepted by the Deaf Community as their own, since they are fluent in ASL and know Deaf Culture well, having grown up in it. But they often struggle with having a foot in each world—the hearing and the deaf—much like I did, as a deaf person raised in a hearing family.

Josh's hands came to rest on his wineglass. He glanced over at Susie to see how she was doing. The little girl was deeply engaged in her art—a drawing of a pony with a little girl sitting on top, signing, "Horse."

"But ever since we had Susie, Gail's changed," Josh continued. "She's become—"

Josh must have noticed my attention switch from his face and hands to someone behind him. He stopped and turned around.

"Hi," Dan gestured and said. Then he signed, "Sorry I'm late," circling a fist on his chest, then waving a hand down at his hip. At that point he gave up signing and just spoke, looking at me to interpret as I lip-read him. "I've been working on this case for the sheriff and had to wait for the results to come back from pathology."

I perked up. "And? What did Arthurlene have to say? Did she identify the body?" I suddenly remembered Susie was there and glanced to see if she was watching me, but she was still working on her picture. I wasn't used to eavesdroppers when I signed, so I'd have to be careful for the little girl's sake. I didn't want to give her nightmares or anything.

Dan looked at me, then at Josh, and reached out a hand. "D-A-N S-M-I-T-H," he finger-spelled. I flushed, embarrassed that I'd forgotten to introduce him a second time.

Josh mouthed the name—or maybe he said it, I couldn't tell—then spelled his own name slowly, sensing Dan didn't know ASL well. Dan repeated Josh's name, and sat down at the end of the table so he could face both of us. Susie glanced up momentarily, eyed him, and he wiggled a few fingers at her. She abruptly returned to her work.

"She hates me," Dan said, nodding toward Susie. Josh and I smiled and shook our heads. Dan signaled the waitress and she made record time getting to the table. Bet she wanted more than Dan's order, the way she was grinning at him. There was something about Dan, his dark hair and multicolored beard, or maybe his hamlike arms and body of steel, that attracted way too many women around here. After dinner I'd leave her a good tip—"Stay away from Dan Smith...."

"Susie's just shy around new people," Josh signed after the waitress returned and left, and I interpreted. Dan took a sip of his Sierra Nevada ale.

"So what did Arthurlene say?" I turned to Josh and briefly explained the discovery that had been made on Buzzard Hill, then returned my attention to Dan.

"It's a dead body, all right," Dan said after a long pull on the beer.

"Very funny. Whose body is it?"

"They don't know yet. But they do have a good idea how old it is."

"A couple of decades?" I guessed. It didn't take long for the buzzards to pick at dead meat around here. Hence the name Buzzard Hill.

"At least a century."

My mouth fell open. This wasn't a dead body. This was practically an archeological find. A valuable relic from the Gold Rush era. My mind flashed on the T-shirts I'd recently seen: ARCHEOLOGISTS JUST PLAIN DIG IT.

"How does Arthurlene know?" I said and signed, when my thoughts cleared.

"Dental work, mostly. She called in Steve Reid, the dentist in town. He's done some forensic dental identification over the years. Apparently skeletons turn up around here more than you'd expect. The procedures for gold teeth used at the time seem to indicate the mid-to-late eighteen-hundreds."

"Wow! I wonder..." I thought for a moment.

"You wonder what?" Dan said.

"Sluice showed me a picture of his great-grandfather while we were up at the site. He thinks the skeleton might be that of his great-grandfather, William Richard Jackson."

Dan shrugged. "I suppose it could be. Rumor has it, the old man ran off with a few bags full of gold and never returned. Then again, could be anyone."

Josh signed, "This area is fascinating. Full of stories like this, isn't it? That's why it's so popular with tourists like me, I suppose."

"Makes great newspaper copy," I signed and said aloud. "Speaking of which, do you have a copy of that report, Dan? I'd like to get the information into the article before it goes to press tonight."

"Nope. Arthurlene won't release it yet. Not until she knows more—such as what exactly happened to him. And who he was, if that's possible to know."

"So, it's a him?"

"That much she does know. The size of the pelvic girdle indicated it was most likely a male."

"Does she have any theories about how the man died?" I signed and said.

Dan took another pull on his beer. It was nearly gone. "Apparently gold isn't the only metal they found in the skull."

"What else? Silver? There was supposed to be quite a lot of silver back then, too."

"Nope, more like lead."

It took a second before the light went on in my head.

Josh still looked puzzled when I finally said, "Wow!"

———◆———

"Do you mind if I pass on dinner?" Dan said, setting the empty bottle on the table after a last swig. He checked his watch again.

"I have a couple more things to do…told Sheriff Mercer I'd do some background work on Chester Orland and get back to him by tonight if I found anything."

I felt a wave of disappointment that he didn't want to stay. Had he given the real reason he was leaving—or was there something else behind it? His body language was ambiguous; his drumming fingers certainly meant anxiety, but over what? The smile of regret looked sincere, but the semi-raised eyebrow appeared to be hiding something more. Dan's face was usually an open book, especially when it came to romance. Tonight it was a mystery novel.

"Yeah, sure," I said, trying not to show my disappointment. I had wanted the two men to get to know each other better.

Josh rose as Dan stood, and the two shook hands. Instead of giving me a quick good-bye kiss as he usually did, he planted one full on. I about fell out of my chair.

"I'll be in my office. See you later?"

I glanced at Josh, a little embarrassed by the display, and pressed my lips together. What was that about? "Well…yes… great. See you there…" I stammered, wide-eyed. What was going on with Dan? Was he suddenly jealous of Josh? Or was it something else…such as guilt? I decided we'd have a talk tonight, for no other reason than to quell an uneasy feeling in the back of my mind.

I watched Dan leave. As soon as he was out of sight, I turned back to Josh. He was staring at me oddly, and suddenly took my hand. An electric current shot up my arm and just about electrocuted me. Where had that come from?

"Connor, it's great seeing you. I don't know what happened to us."

I pulled my hand back and used it to grip my wineglass, more forcefully than I'd intended.

"I guess we just didn't agree on everything back then. Maybe I wasn't deaf enough for you."

Josh shook his head. "No, you were great. I was just too—"

Susie interrupted him, holding up her picture in front of his face. He spent a few minutes discussing the drawing with her in Sign, giving me a moment to think. Three plates of pasta arrived and we didn't talk about anything except general topics—the Mother Lode area, the heat, the gold discovery, Susie's remarkable language skills. My mind was on bodies—the dead one on the hill and the living one in front of me. Josh was still attractive, and I had a strong sense he was still attracted to me. It was flattering, but I had Dan and I was happy with him.

At least I thought I was, until recently, when he'd started acting so strange.

"I'd better get Susie back to the B-and-B," Josh said, waking me from my daydream. "Gail will be after me if I come back too late."

I wondered if they were staying in the same room. I hoped the question didn't sound too obvious when I asked, "Which room did Beau give you?"

"The Roaring Camp Room. It's nice—full of antiques and gold mining stuff."

I found myself a little disappointed to hear they were together, if in fact they were divorced. "That's a great room. Beau's really done a lot to recreate the feeling of the mining days. But my favorite is the Claim Jumpers Room. It's loaded with memorabilia."

Josh looked at his daughter. "Gail and Susie have that room. It's neat, isn't it, Susie?" he signed to her.

So they weren't together after all. I felt a wave of relief pass through me. Wait a minute. Why did I care?

Getting up after dinner we said our good-byes and made

plans to meet in the morning to discuss the cochlear implant for Susie. Susie wanted ice cream but Josh had promised to include Gail for dessert. I recommended the Nugget Café's "Mother Lode Sundae"—chocolate ice cream loaded with chocolate chips and nuts and topped with caramel sauce. Apparently Gail planned to see the audiologist the next morning to discuss Susie's audiogram without Josh. Then they planned to talk over the options and meet with her again later that morning. I wondered why they weren't just going in together, but felt it was none of my business.

Before Josh left, he asked if I could dig up some studies that defended his side of the argument—that an implant might not be the best thing for his deaf daughter. I said I'd look into it. Josh gave my shoulder a squeeze just before he turned to go.

His touch gave me a chill I couldn't identify. Or perhaps I just didn't want to.

—◆—

I rushed up to Dan's office and burst in the door, startling him. He whirled around from the computer.

"Jesus, Connor! You scared the crap—"

He never finished the sentence. His mouth was covered. With mine.

Dan enveloped me in his strong arms and returned the kiss.

"Whoa, where did this come from?" Dan said, finally pulling us apart. He gave me a good once-over, as if he'd never seen this side of me before.

"That waitress at the restaurant," I said, heading in for another kiss. "She made me jealous."

"I think it's the wine," Dan said, laughing. "It's made you insane."

I pulled back. "You don't like it?" I ran my hand down his chest, then slowly pulled his shirt out of his jeans.

He laughed again. "Are we going to have office sex?" he asked, leaning back in his swivel chair and taking it all in as I pulled his T-shirt over his head and threw it across the room.

"We could have hallway sex, if you prefer. Or staircase sex. Or even sidewalk sex…"

"Noooo, no, office sex is just perfect. You want to be the secretary and I'll be the boss?"

I couldn't suppress my smile. "Sure. Now, let me sharpen your pencil.…"

☞ CHAPTER VII.

IT WAS AFTER midnight, and we were really enjoying our office sex when a light from the hall lit up Dan's darkened office. Someone had opened the door. We jumped off the desk, grabbed our clothes, and tried to cover up as we stared at a dark figure in the doorway.

I ducked behind Dan's desk and struggled to pull on my T-shirt. I nearly put my head through the armhole, then readjusted, managing to get the shirt on inside out and backwards. I hiked up my jeans and zipped them closed, nearly catching my skin in the zipper in my haste. I had no idea where my underpants were.

Dan stood half-naked between me and the man in the doorway. He had managed to get his pants back on, which helped him look more menacing. Nothing like a dangling penis to make a man feel vulnerable. Not that I would know.

Dan's back was to me so I couldn't tell what he was saying to the man in the doorway. Considering his strong stance and vigorous gestures, I figured it was something threatening. But the figure in the doorway didn't retreat. In fact, he took a step inside the office. The light from the hall finally illuminated his face. I gasped.

"Sluice! What the hell are you doing here?" I came out from behind the desk and moved next to Dan, who might have said the exact same thing at the exact same time. At least, he looked like he had. We both stood there, hands on hips, waiting for an explanation. I switched on the office light so I could read him better. We all winced at the sudden brightness.

Sluice reached in his overalls pocket and pulled out his nugget. Ambling forward, he held it out toward Dan. Dan didn't reach for it.

"I wanna hire you," Sluice said, placing the nugget on Dan's desk.

Dan picked it up and handed it back to Sluice. "What are you talking about, Sluice? I don't want your nugget. You probably ought to turn it into the sheriff until this mess is cleared up."

"I said, I want to hire you," Sluice said again. "You're a private dick, ain't you?"

Dan sat down on the corner of his desk and gestured for Sluice to take a seat. I took Dan's chair. "What's this all about, Sluice?" Dan said, pulling on his T-shirt. "Why do you want to hire me?"

Sluice drew out the leather-bound photo album from another pocket. I wondered what else he had stashed away in those multi-pocketed overalls. Never mind. I didn't want to know.

Dan went to his mini-fridge and pulled out three Sierra Nevadas. He handed me one, then Sluice, then set his own on the desk and sat down again. Sluice untwisted the cap with his gnarly hands and drank half the beer in one continuous gulp. I glanced at Dan. Even he was impressed.

Wiping the foam from his mouth, Sluice opened the album and showed Dan the picture of the man with the gold front teeth.

"That there's my great-grandpappy, William Richard Jackson. Born 1820. Disappeared 1851."

Dan looked at the picture Sluice had handed him, nodded, then returned it. "It's a little late to fill out a missing person's report, Sluice."

I shot Dan a look for his insensitivity and said, "Sluice, what Dan means is, what exactly do you want him to do?"

Sluice began mumbling a long tale about his ancestors, something about how they came over from Cornwall, England, to make their fortune. I missed a lot of words, but Dan helped me out when I felt I needed clarification. My eyes were about to glaze over from trying to read Sluice's whiskered lips when he finally got to the point.

"Now, my great-grandpappy, William Richard Jackson, and Chesty's great-grandpappy, Orville Orland, discovered gold on Buzzard Hill in 1850. Orville said he owned the land and swore Jack tried to jump the claim. Said Jack came after him with a gun. So he said, anyway."

I glanced at Dan. His interest had been piqued, too. Sluice paused a moment and I wondered if he had nodded off or something. "What happened?" I prompted him.

Sluice blinked his rheumy eyes. "Orville was shot and left for buzzard meat. When they found him, he claimed Jack had run off with a few sacks of gold, afraid he'd be arrested for murder. But Orville recovered just fine—bullet just grazed his ribs."

"And Jack vanished," I said, finishing the story.

Sluice nodded. "No one ever saw my great-grandpappy again."

"I've heard the story, Sluice," Dan said. "It comes up every now and then when the tourists start asking where gold was first found around here. I assumed it was another one of those colorful Mother Lode legends. Still, what is it you want me to do?"

"I ain't done." Sluice finished the rest of his beer, wiped his mouth with his sleeve, and took a deep breath. "Orville Orland's family felt sorry for my great-grandmammy, abandoned in the gold fields with six kids to raise. They took them in and tried to help them get on their feet again."

"That was good of them," I said, but Sluice glared at me.

"Ha! If it was so good, why did the Orlands keep getting richer from their mines, while us Jacksons stayed dirt poor? We were nothing but servants in that house. My great-grandmammy finally started her own laundry business and got away from the Orlands, but she was never more than a few dollars ahead of the poorhouse. She died and left her kids without hardly a penny. One of them kids being my grandpappy."

"What happened to them?" I asked, envisioning alcoholic hoboes, riding the rails and gambling their meager wages away.

"All but two of them died young. Cholera got them. Only my grandpappy and his brother survived to see their twenties. And his brother died the next year in a fall at one of the mines."

Dan and I said nothing. The thought of a whole family being nearly wiped out by disease and tragedy seemed unfathomable.

"When the Orland mine finally ran dry, Orville's son Corning Orland had to sell off all their fancy heirlooms—gold-plated dishes and velvet bedspreads. That's what too much livin' it up'll do. That generation of Orlands ended up with nothing but mined-out land. Corning and his son, Chesty's pappy, Redding, kept searching for another find, but they never did strike pay dirt and died owing huge debts. When Chesty inherited the land, it was pretty much worthless. He couldn't use it as a tourist attraction."

This was the most coherent speech from Sluice I'd ever understood. It must have taken a lot out of him because he seemed to slump further into his chair.

"Nothing ever panned out for Chester, did it?" Dan said.

"Not until now when I found this here nugget on his prop'ty."

Dan stood, a gesture I took to mean, let's wrap this up. We were both tired, and I wanted to get back to my place and maybe finish "taking dictation" from Dan. But Sluice didn't budge. Apparently he wasn't as sensitive to body language as I was.

"I still don't know what you want from me, Sluice," Dan said. He glanced at me for a clue.

"You don't think your great-grandfather really left his family, do you, Sluice?" I asked.

"No, ma'am. He wouldn'ta done that. Jacksons are proud Cornish people. Nothing more important than family."

"So what are you suggesting?" Dan asked.

"Them are my great-grandpappy's bones up there on Buzzard Hill."

Dan didn't seem to know what to say. I took over. "And if that was your great-grandfather, you think…"

"Chesty Orland's great-grandpappy kilt him."

———◆———

Before we could convince Sluice to go home, Dan had to agree to take the case, such as it was. But Dan refused to take the gold nugget.

"I'll pay you, that's a promise," Sluice said as he stood in the doorway about to leave. "I don't take no charity."

Dan nodded. "I'll see what I can find out, Sluice. Now go home and get some rest."

Sluice nodded, but he seemed distracted. I wondered how jumbled his mind really was. Most of the time he seemed to live in a fantasy world, not in touch with the here-and-now. Too much drinking. Always mumbling to himself. Wandering around town aimlessly.

And then he did something that changed my mind about his sanity. He turned around, grinned, and said to me, "You got nice boobies, ma'am."

I thought about slapping him, but as soon as the door closed, I burst out laughing.

—•—

Dan and I reached my diner/home half an hour later and proceeded to complete some unfinished business. I didn't notice the message that must have been slipped under my front door sometime that evening, until I went out to the kitchen to get a glass of water and check on Casper, my hearing ear dog. He had an envelope in his mouth and was chewing on it.

"Give me that!" I said, gesturing for Casper to drop the envelope. He obeyed and I gave him a pat and the sign for "good dog." I picked up the damp paper and saw "Connor Westphal" scrawled across the top. The imprint on the sealed envelope read, MARK TWAIN SLEPT HERE.

Uh-oh. A note from Josh. Apparently he had stopped by sometime after dinner while I was still in the office and I had missed his note, thanks to Casper. What had he wanted? I thought about his touch on my hand: Gesture of friendship? Or something else?

I checked to see if Dan was still awake and found him breathing regularly. Out like a light. Returning to the renovated diner kitchen, I held the note lightly in my hand as I slid into one of the reupholstered booths. Should I open it? I was pretty sure I didn't want to know what it said.

I tore open the envelope and pulled out the sheet of paper with the MARK TWAIN SLEPT HERE letterhead. The handwriting was neat, curving, almost feminine. I read the note slowly.

Dear Connor,

I need your help. As you know, we're in town to see a specialist for Susie. She's a candidate for a cochlear implant and would benefit greatly from the surgery, but Josh—

Josh? I flipped the note over. It was signed Abigail Pike Littlefield. Josh's wife—ex-wife—had written the note! I turned it back over and continued reading:

—but Josh is against the procedure, as I'm sure you can imagine. He hasn't changed much since his college days, defending the rights of the Deaf, and that's why I loved him. But he's become fanatical in his beliefs, to the point where I think his judgment has become impaired—and Susie is paying the price.

I don't know your beliefs about cochlear implants, but I'm hoping you at least have an open mind on the issue. If so, could you possibly talk with Josh and help him see the other side? I'm sure you know the value of being able to hear in a primarily hearing world, and how much Susie would benefit. Josh won't listen to me. He says he knows what's best for Susie, but I think he's wrong. And I know he respects your opinion.

I'm meeting with the audiologist, Delia Thompson, tomorrow at 10:00 in Whiskey Slide. Would you be able to meet me there and hear her side of the story? I've read your newspaper and I, too, respect your opinion. And I hope to gain your support in resolving this important issue.

Sincerely, Abigail Pike Littlefield

P.S. I'd appreciate it if you wouldn't mention this to Josh. He's likely to explode when he finds out I've contacted you behind his back.

I set the note on the table. What an odd request. The woman doesn't even know me and she's asking me to get involved in her personal affairs. Just because I know Josh? Or does she have another motive for getting together with me? She wasn't terribly friendly when I met her this morning. What had changed since then?

Had Josh said something to her about me?

I was truly torn. Josh was my friend, and I understood why he didn't want Susie to have the implant. I also understood Gail's side—it's a hearing world, and deaf people have fewer opportunities because of that, whether we like it or not. Would giving Susie the implant offer her a better life? Or was this a battle between an estranged couple, with Susie a pawn for their own personal agendas?

I hadn't really given the cochlear implant much thought after I'd first read about it. It had been so controversial, and most of the Deaf Community had been skeptical. Then when my parents suggested it, I looked into it, more for their sake, but decided I liked myself the way I was. I didn't miss hearing—how can you miss what you don't know? Besides, I really believe silence is golden. All that noise I see distracting hearing people—loud music, honking horns, "noise pollution"—just looks like a pain in the ear to me.

But what if I had a deaf child and could give her a cochlear implant that would allow her to hear? Would I do it? In a heartbeat.

I was too tired to decide whether to meet Gail or Josh and become embroiled in the situation, or meet neither one and mind my own business. My plate was certainly full enough: I'd promised Sluice to look into his claim about his great-grandfather, there was a pile of bones that needed answers, gold fever was about to hit Flat Skunk, and I had a newspaper to publish.

By morning, my plate had runneth over.

☞ CHAPTER VIII.

WHEN 6:00 A.M. arrived, I was exhausted. Dan woke up so chipper I wanted to smack him. I hadn't slept well, wondering what I should do. After reading Gail's letter and thinking about Josh, I was completely confused. I'd trust my instincts, I guess, as I always had. Most of the time they were right. But not always.

I dragged myself off the sofabed, headed for the shower, while Dan made breakfast and fed Casper. After toweling off I slipped on a blue cotton T-shirt without any words on the front, unusual for me. I wanted to look more professional today—something between just-rolled-out-of-bed and business-casual—if I was going to meet Gail at the audiologist's office. I didn't want her to think I was some small-town reporter who kept her clean laundry in a to-be-hung-up pile and never had anything decent to wear.

"Mocha?" Dan asked, when I entered the kitchen. He handed me a fresh mug with chocolate sprinkles on the top. Casper was lapping up his bowl of water, no sprinkles.

I eyed Dan. "What? Are you trying to bribe me into kitchen sex now?" I took a sip of my drug of choice.

"You're in a testy mood. Didn't sleep well?" Dan sipped his own black coffee as he slid into a booth. I'd renovated the diner's kitchen when I'd moved in, returning it to its fifties splendor, with black-and-white tiles, red Naugahyde upholstery, and stainless steel appliances—just the way my grandparents had it when they opened the place back in 1957. The same year, they'd bought the two-tone red Chevy Bel Air that I'd also acquired after they died. After reading several books set in the fifties, I'd fallen in love with that time period. Life seemed so simple then. Guess that's what I was searching for after moving here from San Francisco—a simpler life. So why did I make things so complicated all the time?

"Connor?" Dan waved a hand in front of my face. I set down the mocha I'd been staring at, as if trying to read my fortune in the chocolate sprinkles, and focused on him. "What's up? Did something happen last night?"

My first thought was of Josh touching my hand. I was sure I blushed. Even though nothing had happened, I still felt guilty for some reason. But no, what was really on my mind was the letter from Gail. I slid out of the booth, retrieved the note from a pile of old mail where I'd dropped it in the middle of the night, and handed it to Dan.

His frown deepened as he read it.

"What's this all about?" He placed the note on the table.

"I told you last night, remember?"

He shrugged and grinned. "I guess my mind was occupied."

I wasn't in the mood for sexy repartee. "The little girl, Susie. Her mother wants her to get a cochlear implant. That's why they're up here, to see a specialist who helped develop the device. But Josh doesn't want her to have it."

"What's a cochlear implant?"

I explained the surgery and device that would enable some deaf people to hear, to varying degrees.

"And they're dragging you into their argument."

I shrugged.

"Don't get involved, Connor. It's their business, not yours. You'll only—"

"I know," I said. "I know. It's just on my mind, that's all."

"Tell them you've got deadlines. A newspaper to run. A man to drive crazy. Whatever. Let them handle it. It's a family issue. I never get involved in family problems. When I was with New York's Finest, domestics were the most dangerous calls of all."

I nodded, resigned to a lecture. But before Dan could continue, he suddenly grabbed at the side of his waist. Appendicitis? He pulled out a cell phone.

While he took the call, I cleared the dishes, checked Casper's doggy door to make sure he could get in and out during the day, and engaged in a brief version of "dish towel tug-of-war" with my husky. Casper won. While Dan wasn't looking, I folded up Gail's letter and tucked it into my backpack. When he finished his call, he looked at me like I'd stolen his wallet. Had he caught me?

He slid out of the booth and wiped his forehead. There would be no let-up in the temperature again today. Although Dan was wearing a cool white T-shirt and jeans, he already looked hot—in more ways than one.

"God, I hate this heat!" I said, plucking at the front of my own T-shirt to let some air in. "You know more murders are committed in hot weather than in cold weather. I read that someplace."

"It's true," Dan said. "Statistically, the higher the temperature rises, the more bodies we find."

I shivered in spite of the heat.

"I'm out of here. See you for lunch?"

I nodded. "Who called?"

Dan shook his head. "Sluice. Wants me to come by his trailer over behind the mortuary. Says he's got something to show me."

"Why are you indulging him?" I asked. "After all, weren't you the one moaning about how busy you are?"

Dan shrugged. "Guess I feel sorry for the old guy. Besides, I've got a little time this morning before I head over to the path lab. The results are supposed to be in before noon."

As soon as he drove away, I grabbed my backpack and was out of there, too. Dan wouldn't have liked what I had planned. But he probably had a good idea what it was.

———◆———

Beau Pascal was sitting in the flower garden of the Mark Twain Slept Here Bed-and-Breakfast Inn, enjoying a latte and one of his famous orange–cranberry rolls. He was so decadent; I was so jealous.

"Connor!" Beau jumped up from his wicker chair when he saw me and gave me a big hug that nearly took my breath away. Granted it had been awhile since I'd seen him—two days. But he was an affectionate guy.

"Hey, Beau. How's the B-and-B business? I'll bet you've got a full house."

I figured he was booked since there were more than the average number of tourists in town—and Josh and Gail were taking up two rooms.

"Yeah, business is good except the guests are running the air-conditioning day and night. I'm going to lose money if this heat doesn't stop. Want a latte and a muffin? I haven't eaten them all yet."

It was a wonder Beau stayed so slim with all his pastry baking. Guess he had that metabolism that allows you to eat a whole pie and not gain any weight. Whereas I eat a lettuce leaf and can't fit into my underpants. I might have to kill him, based on the fact that he looked better in jeans than I did.

"No, actually, I have a question for you. I wondered…you know that couple that checked in yesterday—Josh and Gail Littlefield?"

He rolled his eyes. "God, they're a strange pair. They act like a married couple, bickering all the time, even have a child, but they checked into separate rooms. Oh well, double the money for me."

"Josh is an old friend of mine. He's divorced from Gail, but they're up here to see a specialist for their daughter, Susie. Susie's deaf, too."

He raised an eyebrow. "Old friend, huh? Does this mean Dan's available?'

"In your dreams. Yes, Josh is an old friend, nothing more."

"Yeah, okay. You know it's funny, because at first I thought the whole family was deaf, with all that signing. And then the woman started speaking to me, interpreting for her husband. Glad I didn't call her a bitch out loud!" Beau laughed.

"You think she's a bitch?" I asked.

"Yeah, telling me she wanted clean towels every morning, as if I don't do that. And a bunch of other stuff." Beau hit his chin with the manual letter "B," for "bitch."

"I should never have taught you that sign," I said.

Beau grinned. "You can't imagine how many times I've used it with the more difficult guests around this place. There's another annoying couple who dress in identical clothes every day and drive me crazy with their questions, especially the woman. She constantly wants to know about all my antiques, how old they are, how valuable. I expect half my stuff to be missing when they leave. She gets the 'bitch' sign on a regular basis."

I shook my head sympathetically. Sounded like the Josephs were also staying at the B&B.

"Anyway, I wondered if they were in—Josh and Gail?"

He raised an eyebrow. "I don't know."

"Yeah, right."

"Hey, I don't know half as much about what goes on here as you think I do. Why don't you go knock on their doors and find out?"

I made an I-really-don't-want-to face.

"Oookay. You want me to do it."

I made a that-would-be-great face.

"Hand me that plate of muffins," Beau said, rising. I did, snatching one for myself. "Be right back."

And he was, in about two minutes. He sat down with the plate, still containing the same number of muffins.

"Nobody home?" I asked, doing a bit of mathematical detective work.

"Nope. Or they're not answering their doors."

Hmmm, I thought. Had Gail already left for the audiologist? And where had Josh and Susie gone this morning? "Thanks, Beau. And these muffins are the best."

Guess I'd have to catch up with her at the audiologist's office.

—◆—

I found Delia Thompson's office on the second floor of a two-story medical building, off the main street in Whiskey Slide. Most folks from Flat Skunk take their health needs to Whiskey, since all Skunk has to offer is a Doc-in-the-Box, one of those emergency clinics that provide mostly Band-Aids and bromides. I found her office easily. Her nameplate read DR. DELIA THOMPSON, CCC-A. AUDIOLOGY, SPEECH THERAPY, AND HEARING ASSESSMENT. That meant she was certified in clinical competence in audiology.

I knocked, then waited a polite interval before opening the door. Problem with being deaf is that you never know if someone has said, "Come in." I could have waited out in that hall for hours otherwise.

I expected to see a secretary at a counter and a room full of patients waiting to have their hearing checked, or their speech improved, or their cochlear implants…whatever they do to them. But the room was empty. Then I remembered Delia Thompson was semi-retired and seeing Susie as a favor to Gail. There was only a handful of chairs lining the claustrophobic waiting room, along with a small, unmanned desk. I spotted a closed door and wondered if Gail was already inside talking with the audiologist. Nuts. I had wanted to talk to her before the meeting. I still wasn't sure I was going to go through with this.

I stood for a few minutes, staring at the closed door, hoping the audiologist wasn't deaf and had heard me come in. The sign on the door read SHHH, TESTING IN PROGRESS. After five minutes and five old magazines, a dark-haired woman in her fifties, with horn-rimmed glasses and a sleek bob, opened the inner door and escorted an elderly man out of the room.

No Gail?

I peeked inside the room while Delia Thompson said good-bye to the older gentleman. The walls were covered with white pockmarked acoustic tiles, and a small windowed booth stood at the far end of the room. There was a comfy swivel chair opposite the booth and a console with more buttons than a TV remote.

Delia Thompson turned to face me after closing the door and greeted me with clear words and a smile. She was obviously used to talking with hearing impaired people. She held her hands at her chest, ready to sign if needed, I assumed.

"I'm Connor Westphal. I was expecting to meet someone here…." I glanced around as if Gail might magically materialize.

"Do you have an appointment?" she asked and signed. More than likely she could tell by my voice I was deaf. She leaned over the small desk and pulled open her appointment book. Running her fingers down the column, she looked up, puzzled, when she didn't find my name. "Westphal? The name is familiar, but I don't have you down for today."

"No, no, I was supposed to meet someone here. Gail Littlefield. She has an appointment," I checked my watch, "now, as a matter of fact."

Delia looked again at the appointment book. "No, no Littlefield. I have Gail Pike—"

"Yes, that's her."

"Cochlear implant?" she confirmed.

"Yes, for her daughter, Susie."

"She didn't come with you?"

"No...I went by her place, but she'd already gone. I thought I'd catch up with her here."

"Are you a relative?" she asked.

"No, no. I'm just here—" and why was that exactly? "—for support."

"All right. Would you like a magazine or something while you wait for her?"

"No, thanks," I said, remembering the various "health fad" articles I'd glanced over: liposuction, Botox, eye lifts, implants, and the like. Too depressing. "I'll just wait."

Delia returned to the "Shhh" room, leaving the door open, and made entries in a notebook for the next half hour, while I twiddled my thumbs, cleaned my nails, pushed back my cuticles, went over my chores, scratched every itch I had, and crossed my eyes until I thought they would stick.

No Gail.

About the time I stood up, Delia reappeared. She checked her watch, then glanced at her date book.

"Well, it looks like she's a no-show. And I have another

appointment in a few minutes, so I'd have to reschedule her any-way. When you see her, tell her to give me a call and I'll see if I can squeeze her in later."

I frowned, wondering why Gail hadn't shown up. Had she met up with Josh? Changed her mind?

As I got in my Chevy and drove away, I thought I caught a glimpse of a man and a child, about a block away, walking toward the building. The man's hands waved rapidly in the air, as if he were leading a silent orchestra. The little girl seemed enthralled by his music.

Josh and Susie? What were they doing in Whiskey Slide? I turned the car at the next block and circled around to catch up with them, but they had vanished by the time I got back.

☞ CHAPTER IX.

I PULLED INTO the driveway of the Mark Twain Slept Here and found the front garden deserted. I peeked into the foyer, called Beau's name, waited a few minutes, and gave up. No sign of anyone in the parlor or the hallway. I headed for the Claim Jumpers room to see if Gail was back from wherever she'd gone.

No response to my knock. I didn't bother to try Josh's door. I was pretty sure I knew where he was, but I had no clue where Gail had disappeared to. Odd, since she'd said she wanted to meet with me. I had an uneasy feeling about her.

Back at the office I checked over this morning's edition of the *Eureka!* and found fewer-than-average errors. Miah, my office help, had done a good job of proofreading. All I'd have to do for the next edition was correct the switched captions on a couple of photos, since the picture of Jilda Renfrew holding up her prize-winning fingernails on page four was certainly not PETUNIA, WORLD'S BIGGEST PORKER.

By the time I had finished fiddle-farting with the changes, it was time for lunch. I felt drenched and ready for a cool beer. Time to meet Dan for a BLT at the Nugget.

As usual, the place was packed at noon, but Dan must have

come early. He'd already staked a claim at a booth in the middle of the crowded diner. The number of tourists in town seemed to be rising as fast as the temperature. Had the "fever" already spread beyond the Mother Lode?

"You're a saint!" I said, sliding in opposite him. He had a Sierra Nevada waiting for me. I chugged a third of it before I said another word. "God, it's hot in here!"

He nodded at the obvious. The Nugget Café didn't have air-conditioning either and the window fans were spinning at full capacity. Dan's beard sparkled with tiny beads of sweat and I wondered why he didn't shave off the fuzz in this blistering weather. Surely it made him even warmer. I wondered what he'd look like without the beard, then shook my head. I didn't want him to change a thing.

"What?" he said.

"What?" I answered.

"You shook your head. What's wrong?"

I grinned at being caught thinking about him. "Nothing. I was just picturing you...without—"

"My clothes?"

I apparently laughed so loudly I caught the attention of both the booths on either side of us. I scrunched down, self-conscious, and waited for the distracted diners to return to their meatloaf sandwiches and Hangtown Fry.

"Is that all you ever think about?" I hissed, taking my embarrassment out on him.

"Pretty much," he said. Suddenly I got the feeling he was picturing me naked.

"What? Now you want to have Nugget Café sex?" I hoped I was whispering. His eyes seemed to sparkle. Maybe it was sweat.

"Well, stop it!" I ordered. "Tell me how your chat with Sluice went."

Jilda stopped by, glared at me, then held up her newspaper picture with the pig caption. I apologized profusely for the error and promised her it would be fixed by the next edition. She brusquely took our orders—a BLT and a grilled cheese—and left with a final stinging look.

"What was that about?" Dan said, idly picking up his beer.

"Nothing. Just a common newspaper error. Miah switched a couple of photo captions. Made Jilda look like a pig. So what about Sluice?"

Dan took a swig and set the bottle down. "You know Sluice. Half the time I had no idea what he was talking about. He wanted to show me some of his great-grandfather's things, but they didn't mean much to me. I don't know what's going on in that head of his."

"Neither do I. But I feel sorry for the guy. He's convinced those Buzzard Hill bones are his great-grandfather's," I said. "So what does he want you to do about it?"

"I don't know. He thinks because I'm an investigator I can conjure up some kind of proof that it's his ancestor."

"What did you tell him?"

"What I told him before. I'd look into it. Then he started rambling on about something else."

"Important?"

"Who knows? Something about a fight last night, disturbing his beer-drinking here at the Nugget."

"In this heat, I'm surprised there haven't been more fights breaking out."

Jilda arrived, two plates balanced on her arm. She set them in front of us, her freshly decorated nails part of the presentation, then quickly left before I could say, "Wait a minute! This isn't what I ordered!"

Dan got his grilled cheese, but in front of me sat a PB&J

sandwich. Not even close to a BLT. Guess that'll teach me to ac-cidentally call Jilda a pig.

I took a bite and gave her a peanut-butter smile from across the room. She sneered back. When I could finally open my sticky mouth again, I said, "Where were we?"

"Sluice."

I swallowed the gummy mass and rinsed it down with beer. I hadn't had a PB&J since I was twelve. And now I remembered why.

"So what was this fight about? Did it have anything to do with Sluice and his recent find?"

"I don't think so. The way he described it, it sounded like it had something to do with your friend, what's his name?"

I gave him a blank look.

"The deaf guy. Apparently he and his wife and kid were in here late last night."

"Really?" Then I remembered that Josh and Susie had planned to meet Gail for dessert.

"I guess. Sluice said it was right around closing time. Must have been about ten or so. He said there were only a couple of guys, him, and the deaf people."

"Gail's not deaf, remember. So what did he say happened?" With the mention of Josh and Gail, he had piqued my interest. I started to take another bite of the sandwich, then thought better of it and took a bite of Dan's grilled cheese instead.

"He said their hands were flying like crazy. Said the man—Josh—looked really angry, did most of the 'hand waving,' as Sluice called it. I think it kind of spooked him. He thought may-be they were talking about him, plotting to take his gold nugget away. He got up and left, taking his beer with him."

"That's ridiculous!"

"You know Sluice. That's the way he thinks. He's always been kind of paranoid. He's even more mistrustful, now that he's found that nugget."

"Was Josh...violent?" I asked.

"Sluice didn't say. Just said he didn't want to hang around."

I thought about the semi-public fight between Josh and Gail. I'm sure it was about the cochlear implant. It was an emotional issue and likely to bring out the worst in both parents. Poor Susie, caught in the middle of it all. I felt for her.

Still, it didn't explain what had happened to Gail this morning—why she didn't show up for her appointment. Maybe Josh finally talked her out of the procedure and went to the audiologist himself, to explain why they weren't going to go ahead. Maybe Gail was still angry from the fight, packed up in a huff, and left. Maybe she just didn't want to deal with the whole thing anymore. Or with Josh and his temper. I remembered a few outbursts he'd had during college, but that was because of his passion over some issue. And he never really crossed the line back then. Had he changed over time?

Between the two of us, the grilled cheese disappeared quickly, and we gave up the booth moments later, leaving room for the next hungry gold diggers to take our place. Dan and I split up outside, he headed for the coroner's office, while I wavered between going back to work or going back to the B&B. I wanted to check on Gail one last time before I gave up. Maybe Josh had browbeaten her into changing her mind and she could use support. Oh, let's face it—I was just plain curious about what had happened between them.

Beau was in the garden, wearing a big straw sun hat, a turquoise tank top, and khaki shorts. You'd think he'd have acquired some color after working out in the sun, but his skin remained lily white, dotted with tiny freckles. He had a tall lemonade next to him that looked inviting, even after the cold beer.

"Hey Beau, it's too hot to be gardening. Why aren't you cooling off in your spa? I assume you're not heating it in this weather."

Beau turned around. "I can't sit still, you know that. Besides, working in the garden is peaceful. I've got lots of shade to keep me cool."

I glanced around for a sign of Gail or Josh.

"You come looking for your friends again?" he said, chopping at a prickly thing with a trowel.

"Yeah, I thought I'd check on Gail. See if she's back yet."

"Feel free. But I haven't seen her come in or go out. Your man friend, either."

"Thanks." I headed down the hall and rapped on Gail's door, hoping she'd answer this time. I called her name, thinking if she wasn't answering the door to Josh after their fight, maybe she would to me. No such luck. I was about to turn and go when I decided to try the doorknob. Locked. That would have been too easy. I headed back to the garden and found Beau sipping his lemonade.

"Nobody home?" he said, setting down the drink.

"No, and I'm kind of worried. Did you see either of them come in last night? Especially Gail?"

"No, can't say that I did. But I was watching 'Six Feet Under.' You think there might be some sort of trouble or something?" Beau loved drama and created it whenever he could.

"I don't think so, but could you check on her, just to make sure?" I asked. "I don't want to invade her privacy, but if you could take a peek inside…"

Beau stood up and brushed the dirt off his butt and knees. "Let me get the key." He returned in a few moments with an old-fashioned, gold-painted key attached to a fake gold nugget. I followed him down the hall to Gail's room, remembering the last time I had entered one of Beau's rooms unannounced. I'd received the shock of my life—what I thought was the body of a dead woman—and I didn't relish a repeat of that scenario.

Beau knocked twice, waited a moment, then inserted the key, twisted the knob, and slowly inched the door open. He called out something like "Anybody home?" I couldn't quite make out his words, but I figured that's what he was saying.

He pushed the door another inch. I could feel the hairs on the back of my neck tingle. As he shoved the door open the rest of the way, his eyes widened and his mouth dropped open. I peered inside.

The room was empty.

The bed had been made—or not slept in. The drawers and armoire were cleaned out. There was no sign of a suitcase. In fact, there was nothing to indicate the room had ever been occupied.

Beau turned to me and frowned.

"That's odd. She didn't check out. And they've paid for two more nights. Where do you suppose she is?" he said.

I had absolutely no idea.

But I had a feeling I'd better find Josh.

☞ CHAPTER X.

THE LAST I'D seen of Josh was in Whiskey Slide, on his way to see the audiologist. At least, I thought it was Josh I had spotted headed down the street, signing with Susie. I wondered if there was any chance he might still be there. Maybe he'd had a change of heart and wanted to discuss the cochlear implant with the audiologist. Maybe he was meeting Gail there. Maybe—

Enough supposition. I had to drive out there. What other choice did I have except waiting around here? I couldn't exactly call him on his cell phone. If I didn't catch him there, maybe I could find out from Delia Thompson where he was headed next. Or if Gail had ever shown up.

The twenty-minute drive took thirty, thanks to the recent influx of extra tourists. I opened the Chevy's windows and caught as much cool air as I could. I felt the sweat trickling under my T-shirt. Truthfully it felt good. When I caught the air just right through one sleeve, I managed to create a draft throughout my entire shirt. Who needed air-conditioning when that swirling air hit the trickling sweat?

I didn't know what kind of car Josh drove, so I couldn't check outside to see if he was parked near the medical building. Glancing up and down the main street, I saw no sign of him, so to speak. I parked the Chevy and headed up the stairs to Delia's office, entering without knocking this time. The audiologist sat behind her front desk going over papers. She looked surprised to see me again. Or was that irritation?

"Hi," I said, moving in tentatively.

She smiled. "Are you still looking for your friend?" she asked and signed.

"Yes. Uh, no. Actually, I was looking for Josh this time. I wondered if he had an appointment with you, too. I thought I saw him with his daughter headed this way." I glanced through the open door of the testing room, but the place seemed empty.

"Yes, he had an appointment."

"He's gone?"

"They left about half an hour ago."

"Did he say where they were going?"

"No, sorry. Is it important?"

Turning point. I could either make up a story—which I'm good at—or tell the truth—which I'm not so good at. What would benefit me the most? I compromised. I'd give her a little of both.

"Do you mind if I ask you a couple of questions, Dr. Thompson? For my newspaper? I'd like to help the public better understand the latest developments for the hearing impaired. Naturally I have an interest, being deaf."

I sat down in the chair opposite her to read her better, although she was a speech-reader's dream. She spoke slowly and clearly, without exaggeration, and used a lot of facial expression to give her words just the right nuance. If only everyone spoke like Delia Thompson.

"I suppose, but I can't really talk about my patients. That's confidential."

"I understand. No, it's more for my own information and for the newspaper. About the cochlear implant. I was going to interview Josh and Gail, but I wanted to get your viewpoint, too."

Delia straightened herself as if preparing for a long, defensive explanation of the procedure. I interrupted her before she began her spiel.

"I know all about the surgery and what it's supposed to do. I mostly want to know what you think about the C.I. As an audiologist, do you really feel the procedure is a good thing for a deaf person?"

"Of course. I helped develop it," she said firmly. "Giving a deaf person the opportunity to hear? Who wouldn't want that?"

"Perhaps a deaf parent of a deaf child," I said. "Did you see the documentary 'The Sound and the Fury'? It was about a deaf couple trying to decide whether or not their daughter should—"

She cut me off. "Get an implant. Of course, I've seen it. But that was just one couple. They don't represent the entire Deaf Community. And they only interviewed one family who'd had the procedure done on their child. The parents were hearing, so naturally they were biased."

She pulled back in her chair and looked down at her papers, as if trying to compose herself. The issue seemed to cause an emotional reaction in some people. She took a deep breath and began again. "Look, I understand how a deaf parent might feel—"

"Do you?" I said, cutting her off. I tried not to look accusingly at her, but it was difficult.

"All right, probably not completely. But I have had some experience with the Deaf Community. My parents were both deaf."

"You're a CODA?"

She frowned. "I'm not exactly a 'child of a deaf adult,' as it's defined. My parents became deaf as they got older."

"Degenerative deafness due to aging, like presbycusis or tinnitus? That's not the same thing."

"You're right, but it wasn't just aging. They both had a genetic disease called Usher Syndrome."

As I understood it, Usher Syndrome is a genetic disorder that's responsible for ten percent of the deaf population. Some also have problems with balance and vision. I had met a wonderful man with Usher Syndrome who owned a Cajun restaurant in Seattle, even though he was profoundly deaf and nearly blind. He'd been such an inspiration to me, I had written my first real journalism piece about him.

When I regained my speech, I asked the obvious question. "Both of your parents have Usher? Isn't that incredibly rare?"

She nodded as if this were a routine question and she was tired of answering it. "It's a long story. My parents met in an Usher support group when they were in their thirties. My father was divorced at the time and my mother was still single. They hit it off and eventually got married. They certainly had something in common and understood what their futures would be like, having Usher Syndrome. But it didn't stop them from falling in love and having a family."

"But, since the disease is genetic, they must have known their chances of passing it on were high—" I stopped, suddenly embarrassed at the personal probing I'd been doing. I'd experienced similar questions myself and thought them rude. People always assumed I would never have children in case I might pass on my deafness. Since mine was caused by meningitis, that would have no genetic effect on my future children.

"You mean, what are the chances of my having Usher syndrome and becoming deaf—and possibly blind — too?"

I nodded sheepishly and thought immediately about her job. She would no longer be able to function as an audiologist.

"Zero."

I frowned and sat back. "Zero? Have you been tested?"

"I'm adopted."

I nodded slowly, feeling like a fool. It all made sense. I could imagine how it might have played out. After her parents married, they adopted her, to avoid giving birth to a child with Usher Syndrome. Growing up in that family, she must have decided to study audiology.

"So, since your parents probably weren't really part of the Deaf Community, per se, you aren't really a CODA."

"My parents were great. They had each other, of course, but it was very difficult for them. And hard for me, too. I had to step up as interpreter and do a lot of things most children don't have to do or talk about."

I'd heard it before from many children of deaf adults. Having to take on the responsibility of hearing for their parents was a job that sometimes interfered with their childhoods and forced them to grow up fast, whether they liked it or not.

"I saw how deafness affected my parents, slowly, over time. That's why I'm so encouraged by the C.I. If I can give the gift of hearing to anyone—young, old, prelingual, postlingual, severely deaf, or just hard of hearing, I'd do it."

"Is the procedure really safe?" I asked, thinking of Susie. "For a child?"

"About one in ten deaf kids today has an implant, and there have been no negative aftereffects. We expect one in three will have them in the next ten years."

"In other words, as far as you know, it's safe. And growing in acceptance and popularity."

"Most deaf children are born to hearing parents. Those parents definitely want their children to hear, if they have the opportunity."

"But some deaf people don't feel the same way," I added.

"Yes, it may be threatening to some members of the Deaf Community."

"Like Josh."

Delia said nothing. I was broaching the confidentiality issue. I'd have to be more careful and try another tack.

"If a deaf parent, say, was adamantly against the C.I. for his deaf child, but the hearing spouse was for it, what would you advise?"

"That's really a decision the two of them have to make."

"But you'd encourage the implant, right?"

"I would tell them all the pros and cons of the procedure and let them make their own decision."

"And what if they couldn't come to a decision?"

"Then we'd have an impasse, wouldn't we," she said. "Unless something happens to change one of the parents' minds, the child will continue to be caught in the middle of a very emotionally charged debate."

As I stood up to go, Delia raised her index finger. "Do you mind if I ask you a personal question?"

I shook my head. After all, I felt I owed her one.

"Have you ever considered getting an implant yourself?"

"Sure, I've thought about it. But I like—"

"You like being deaf? So many deaf adults tell me that—they like being deaf. How would they know the difference since they haven't experienced hearing? I think it's just plain fear."

"I wasn't going to say I like being deaf. I was going to say I like myself the way I am. And I don't think it's fear. It's just acceptance. Anything wrong with that?"

Delia shrugged. She'd probably tried once too often to argue with a stubborn Deafie like me and had learned to give up quickly. Since I had nothing left to say, I thanked Delia for her time and information and promised to let her know when the article would appear. I had no idea, since I wasn't planning on writing one, but the more I delved into the topic, the more interesting and controversial it became. It was the stuff of newspapers.

On the drive back to Flat Skunk, I wondered where Josh and Susie were. And Gail, for that matter. I planned to swing by the B&B and see if I could catch Josh. I seemed to be two steps behind everyone today. Must be my shoes.

When I arrived at the Mark Twain, I was surprised to see the sheriff's patrol car there, along with a backup from Whiskey Slide. The car doors were ajar; no one inside. A small collection of guests on the front porch talked among themselves, including the matching archeologists. I caught a glimpse of Beau chatting with a good-looking guy just inside the foyer. I could tell by the look on Beau's face that something had happened at the inn. And it probably wasn't good. I got a tingle at the back of my neck.

I pushed my way through the group to Beau.

"Oh, Connor! You're all right! I was so worried!" He gave me one of his chest-crushing hugs.

"Why were you worried about me? What's going on here?" I indicated the swelling crowd. Sheriff Peyton Locke from Angels Camp stood sentry at the front of the hall, keeping the guests at bay. I waved at her, but she didn't acknowledge me. Official police business and all that, I figured.

I looked back at Beau to read his lips. He was already talking. "...and you were with him, so I told Sheriff Mercer, and he went barreling in—"

"Whoa! What are you talking about? Start over."

"They found your friend," Beau said.

"Who? Josh?"

"Gail," Beau said.

"Where was she? I thought she'd left the inn."

Beau said nothing and couldn't meet my eyes. The tingling at the back of my neck turned to a chill down my spine.

"Beau? What is it? Has something happened to her?"

Before he answered me, Josh came out of his room at the end of the hall, looking as if he'd seen a dead body. As he moved toward me, I saw Sheriff Mercer walking right behind him.

"What's going on?" I signed to Josh as he approached me and the gawking group.

Josh didn't raise his hands to sign to me. When he passed by, I saw why. He couldn't. His hands were cuffed behind his back.

He turned back to face me just before Sheriff Mercer stuffed him into the back seat of his patrol car. Even though he couldn't talk with his hands bound, his facial expression said plenty:

"Help me, Connor."

I looked at Beau for answers as Sheriff Mercer took Josh away.

"Why did they arrest him? What did he do?"

Beau looked pained and touched my arm. "His wife—ex-wife—she was found dead."

I froze. I felt the blood drain from my head. I had to hold onto Beau to fight the dizziness and keep from losing my balance. Gail? She couldn't be dead. I'd gotten that note....

"When?"

"About an hour ago."

"How?"

"They didn't say."

"Where?"

"In the trunk of a car." Beau gave my arm a squeeze. The dizziness swept over me again. I had a feeling I didn't have to ask whose car.

☞ CHAPTER XI.

I STARED AT Beau, stunned at the news. There was no way Josh could be responsible for Gail's death, no matter how much evidence they might have against him. Even though they were divorced and they disagreed on Susie's future, he wouldn't kill anyone, especially not the mother of his child.

He just wouldn't.

"Happens all the time," Beau said, reading my mind.

I gave him a harsh look.

He shrugged it off. "Domestic violence is the number one cause of murder. You're more likely to be whacked by someone you know than by a stranger."

"What, are you a cop now?"

"No, but I watch 'Cops' on TV. You learn a lot on that show," he said defensively.

"You're just watching it to see those men in uniform," I said.

"Maybe. But I still learn a lot. And I'm right about domestic disputes. Just ask Sheriff Mercer. Or Dan." Already had, thank you.

I suddenly realized something was missing. Actually, some*one*.

"Where's little Susie?" I glanced around the area.

"She's in the backyard with Deputy Clemens. They're waiting for Social Services."

Oh, God. The poor girl. Her mother dead, her father accused of murder. Being deaf, she was sure to be confused about what was going on. I'd try to be with her when Social Services arrived and interpret as best I could.

But a government car pulled up before I could go and check on Susie. I met the woman as she exited the car and started to introduce myself when I recognized her.

"Victoria Serpa," I said.

"Westphal, isn't it?" she replied. "The Jonathan Samuels case last year. Are you involved in this case, too?"

I explained my relationship to Josh and why I'd wanted to be with Susie when Social Services arrived—to act as interpreter and offer support. Victoria Serpa seemed to have no problem with my being there. Together we headed for the backyard where we found Susie studying some frogs in one of Beau's many ponds.

I nodded at Deputy Clemens, then explained to Susie as gently and simply as I could that her mother and father would be gone for a while and that the nice lady was going to take care of her until her daddy came back. She nodded to indicate she understood, looking terrified and on the verge of tears.

I wished I could sweep her up in my arms and take her home.

After waving good-bye to Susie, I hopped in my Chevy and headed for the sheriff's office to find out what the hell was going on.

"What the hell is going on?" I said, bursting in the door.

Rebecca Mathews, the octogenarian dispatcher, nearly dropped the flower pot she was painting red, white, and blue. Rebecca was always working on some crafty project to kill time between 911 calls. This time it was patriotic pot painting. No doubt something for the annual craft boutique to be held on the upcoming Labor Day holiday. She gave me a disgusted look, as if to blame me for making her current white star look more like bird poop.

Sheriff Mercer, on the other hand, seemed to be expecting me. He didn't jump, startle, or even look up from his paperwork.

"Good afternoon to you, too, C.W."

"What the hell is going on?" I faced him across his desk. He had to look up now.

He put his pen down and folded his hands behind his head. "We've made an arrest for a homicide. If you want the details for your newspaper, they'll be released later this afternoon."

"No, I don't want the details for my newspaper. The man you arrested is a friend of mine, Josh Littlefield. I want to know what happened."

The sheriff pulled his fingers apart and spread his hands on his desk. After a big sigh, he started to explain. "We found the body of Abigail Pike Littlefield, Joshua Littlefield's wife—"

"Ex-wife," I corrected.

"Ex-wife, in the trunk of his blue late-model Honda Accord parked at the Mark Twain Slept Here Inn. His prints are on the car, his wife's purse, and the murder weapon, also found in the trunk."

"Which is?"

"A big rock. A large chunk of iron pyrite, to be exact."

I couldn't believe his lips. "Fool's gold?"

"Yep. Blow to the head. At least, that's what we think happened. Body's over at Arthurlene's for an autopsy."

"And based on this slim circumstantial evidence, you think Josh killed his ex-wife."

"Apparently they had an argument at the Nugget Café before she died. A big one, according to my source."

"And who would your source be? Sluice Jackson, who's at worst incompetent and at best incoherent most of the time?"

"Anonymous caller."

"What?"

"Got a call about an hour and a half ago. Someone said to look in the trunk of Josh's car. Had some other details, too."

"How did this anonymous caller know all this stuff? Did you ever think the caller might be the killer?"

"Thought about it. But there's too much evidence against your friend. The caller said he saw the whole thing but was too scared to do anything except notify us."

"Do you have the voice on tape? Can you identify it?"

Sheriff Mercer shook his head and tapped his ear. "Called my cell, which is pretty fuzzy."

"The caller knew your cell number? Don't you find that odd?"

"Not necessarily. I've passed it out to a quite a few folks, in case they needed me while I was out in the field. Could have been anyone."

"And you didn't recognize the voice?" I knew the sheriff was losing his hearing, but maybe he could still make out the identity of the caller.

"Like I said, too much static," he said. "Male, maybe."

I shook my head. How was all this possible? Gail was dead. Josh was in jail. Susie was in protective custody. And the world had turned upside down.

I took a breath, tried to compose myself, and sat down in the chair opposite the sheriff. "What are you going to do?"

"Nothing right now. Wait for the autopsy."

"Does Josh have a lawyer?"

"I let him use our TTY to call someone. I think he called that Deaf referral agency—they're sending someone. Not a lot of deaf lawyers in these parts, you know. It may take a while."

"Can I see him?"

I could see Sheriff Mercer's brain trying to come up with an excuse to keep me out of the picture. After a few seconds, he gave up. "All right. But make it short."

I followed the sheriff to the back of the office where he kept prisoners in two cells. Josh lay on the no-frills cot staring up at the ceiling, his hands behind his head. He sat up quickly when he noticed our presence.

"Connor," he signed. "Thank God!"

"What happened?" I kept our conversation in sign language without speech so the sheriff couldn't eavesdrop. He soon grew bored and left us alone.

"I don't know! One minute I'm having a great time with my daughter, the next I'm in jail. They say I killed Gail. It's not true!" His signs were sharp and forceful, full of emotion. "God! I can't believe she's dead!"

"I know it isn't true. But the sheriff says he's got some evidence. Have you got a lawyer?"

"DCARA is sending someone from Fremont. But what about Susie?"

"She's fine. She's with Social Services. They'll take care of her until you're out of here."

Josh rubbed his forehead. "No. Not Social Services. I've had too many encounters with them. They don't understand Deaf people. They're always trying to make us fit into the hearing world."

He couldn't stop being political, even when his freedom was in jeopardy.

"Susie will be fine. She's a strong, intelligent girl." I signed it, but I wasn't sure I meant it. I'd had my dealings with Social Services over the years, too, and although they tried to do what was best for their clients, their hands were too often tied up in bureaucratic rules and regulations.

"Connor, please. Can you take her? Just until I'm out of here? Please?" He made the sign for "please" on his chest, with impassioned circles.

"I don't think they'll let me. Don't you have a relative or someone who could take her?"

Josh shook his head. "No, only some distant relatives on Gail's side who she barely knows. Please, Connor. I know she'd be happier with you."

"I'll see what I can do. It's an involved process with lots of red tape, as you know."

"I'd feel so much better if I knew she was with you instead of some hearing strangers."

"Well, let's concentrate on getting you out of here. Talk with your attorney, tell him everything, and I'll do what I can to find out more about this mysterious anonymous caller who seems to be a convenient eyewitness."

I finally left Josh, promising to do what I could about both Susie and his situation. He still looked worried to death when the sheriff escorted me out.

And I still couldn't believe Gail was really dead.

The first thing I wanted to know was how Gail was discovered and the condition of her body, but I knew I wouldn't find out anything until the autopsy results were in. I could check in with Dan and share the latest news, although he'd probably heard it already from half the townspeople. Or I could try to find out who that caller was.

But where to begin?

With the only real clue I had to go on: the person who had overheard the fight between Gail and Josh last night.

Sluice Jackson.

☞ CHAPTER XII.

I FELT THE first breezes of oncoming evening whisper against my flushed cheek as I left the sheriff's office. I checked my watch and was surprised to see how late it had become. I'd missed dinner completely and wondered if Dan had been looking for me. We often met for pasta at my house when the day's work was finished. Just like an old married couple.

Now it was after seven, and I felt I'd accomplished little, thanks to the many distractions throughout the day. I wondered how Dan had fared with Arthurlene. I decided to swing by his office on the chance that he was still there, before I headed for Sluice's usual haunts: The Nugget, The Library—which was the name of a popular bar—or the gazebo in the middle of the town, where he hung out, drank from paper-bagged bottles, or hawked his beaded jewelry that was pinned to his frayed old cap. I was sure it wouldn't be long before he'd be selling GOLD! emblazoned caps, with little fake nuggets glued to the visors. The tourists were suckers for anything related to gold.

Dan wasn't in his office, and his door was locked. I left a note, telling him of my plans and that I'd meet him back at my diner later if he wanted to come over. I went searching for Sluice, but he was missing from his hangouts and no one had seen him for several hours. I knew one last place to check—his trailer. Sluice was a part-time caretaker at the Memory Kingdom Mortuary, so the owner, Del Rey Montez, had given him the old abandoned trailer parked in the back to live in. It wasn't much, but it was free, as Sluice often said.

The walk to the Memory Kingdom Mortuary from the middle of town is short, but the change in scenery is dramatic. The buildings of Flat Skunk end abruptly after five short blocks, at Jail Street, where the landscape returns to its native flora. Scrub brush, oaks, manzanita bushes, and pine trees line the street, breaking only for the mortuary driveway that rises up a small grade. Tonight the parking lot was empty, the lights were off in the mortuary home, and the landscape lighting gave an eerie glow in the growing twilight.

I made my way over the well-kept lawns to the cemetery plots in the back, carefully avoiding stepping on any graves. You never knew when a hand might grab your ankle. I'd learned that from watching too many horror movies. I walked by my grandparents' markers, sent them a smile, and kept moving toward the back of the lot.

The cemetery grew gloomier by the minute as I made my way, and I was tempted to speed up my pace before it became too dark to see. Take away a deaf person's most important sense—sight—and watch us get more than a little anxious. The light from the trailer windows shone dimly through the filth of the glass, but at least I figured Sluice was home.

"Sluice!" I called, pounding on the peeling wooden door. The makeshift trailer had been built by hippies decades ago from the wood that was abundant in these parts. It was abandoned for years until Del Rey's ex-husband rented it for a short time. Then it had gone to Sluice as partial payment for his caretaking work. The place should have been condemned, but then Sluice wouldn't have had anywhere to sleep except the downtown gazebo.

I wiped the grunge off my knuckles and waited for him to open up. "Sluice! It's me, Connor!" I pounded again. Nothing.

Maybe he wasn't home after all.

Out of the corner of my eye, I thought I saw a shadow moving beyond the trailer. "Sluice?" I called out and waved. Maybe he was outside taking a leak. But the shadow disappeared.

Not Sluice? My heart sped up. My palms broke out in a sweat.

I thought about the zombies in *Night of the Living Dead*.

I thought about that dead cat in *Pet Sematary*.

I thought I saw the shadow move again, farther away in the distance.

I was freaking myself out.

I wiped my hands on my pants, gently tried the slippery doorknob, then grasped it forcefully and turned. The handle gave. Had it been unlocked and just stuck? Or had I broken the handle in my panic to get inside?

Where it was safe.

I opened the door a crack.

Please let Sluice be home. Even if he wasn't much protection, at least I could lock the trailer door behind me and stay there until—what?

I called his name again, not wanting to startle him, then pushed the door to open it fully.

Something stopped it from opening more than an inch.

I shoved it again, this time using my shoulder. It gave another inch. There was just enough room for me to peer inside and see what was blocking the door's path.

A body.

Sluice lay sprawled on his stomach on the floor of the trailer. A little blood had trickled and dried on the side of his head. I squatted down and pushed at his torso, trying to ease him out of the way. Between shoving the body with my foot and pushing on the door with my shoulder, I managed to clear enough space to squeeze inside.

I stepped over Sluice's apparently lifeless body and knelt down to take his pulse.

He didn't look like he was breathing.

Until he rolled over and threw up on my Doc Martens.

"Sluice!" I sprang up, not knowing whether to be angry or relieved. I went with relief at his being alive, first, then I'd let him have it for ruining seventy-five-dollar shoes. Now I had a good excuse to get those new ones. I knelt down again and called his name. He reeked of alcohol and vomit.

Sluice tried to lift his head again, this time to look at me, I hoped. It was too much of an effort. His face slammed back to the floor. I glanced around the trailer for a phone, hoping to call an ambulance. Who was I kidding? The guy didn't even have cable, let alone a phone.

"Sluice!" I patted his cheek, hoping to rouse him. "What happened? Were you hit?" I tried to roll him over, but he was a dead weight, so to speak. I began to panic. I couldn't possibly carry him out of the trailer. I could run to the mortuary for help, but there was that shadow I was sure I'd seen, lurking around. What if it was responsible for Sluice's injury?

I got up and searched for some kind of clean cloth to attend to Sluice's head wound and found nothing that wasn't caked or riddled with dried food, dirt, or billions of microscopic germs. I didn't want him getting cholera or anything, so I pulled off my T-shirt, ran it under the tap in the "kitchen"—meaning a sink and hot plate—and applied it to the gash on his head. He didn't seem to notice the pain as I gently wiped the wound clean. No wonder. I quickly saw the cut was only superficial, barely a scrape.

But what had happened? I looked around for an answer and found what I assumed was the weapon.

A beat-up coffee table stood inches away from a worn-out couch. Together the two pieces of furniture pretty much filled up the tiny room. There was blood on the corner of the table near Sluice's head. Right about where you'd hit it if you were literally falling down drunk. Which Sluice seemed to be. There was an empty bourbon bottle under the table that wasn't visible when I first arrived. Now the situation was more than clear.

Sluice rolled over. I about fainted from the smell of toxic fumes coming from his mouth, and stood up again.

"You're drunk and you fell!" I said, mostly to myself. He was long past listening. "You haven't been attacked. You must have passed out and hit your head on the table corner." Exasperated, I plopped down on the threadbare couch against the wall, then wished I hadn't. There was something wet under my butt. Could be alcohol. Could be worse. I leapt back up.

Sluice was dead to the world. How much had he had? Just the one bottle? That would have been enough to kill me, but apparently not Sluice, whose tolerance must be measured in vats by now. Of course, the fall could have killed him. He'd been lucky this time.

I had to get out of there. I needed fresh air, clean clothes, a shower—and new shoes. But I felt bad leaving the old guy lying on his bare wood floor. I shoved the small table aside, then spent the next fifteen minutes trying to drag Sluice's dead weight over to the couch and shove him up onto the cushions. It would have been easier pushing a wheelbarrow full of bricks up Buzzard Hill.

Before I left, I covered him with an old, torn Barbie sleeping bag, something he must have retrieved out of a Dumpster. I was sure I had a couple of blankets I could bring him in the morning. I'd had no idea he lived so meagerly. In spite of the smell and the filth, my heart went out to him. Poor old guy.

I thought of the bones he claimed belonged to his great-grandfather. At least I could help him determine whether or not they were the remnants of his long-lost relative. At least, when I wasn't trying to clear Josh for murder, find out who killed Gail, and see about taking care of little Susie. I thought about slipping on my bloody shirt, then decided, the hell with it—Sluice could keep the shirt. No one was likely to see me in my bra now that it was dark out.

Except maybe that shadow.

—◆—

I found Dan waiting for me at my diner when I returned. He was watching captioned TV and having a beer on my couch. He switched off the TV with the remote and stood up to greet me.

"Hi!" I said, glad to see him, and gave him a hug.

"What's that smell?" he said, pulling away and making a face.

I looked down. Apparently I had gotten used to the smell. "My shoes."

"You need to see a podiatrist about that," he said, scrunching up his nose.

"I don't have foot odor. It's puke!"

"Where did you get the puke?"

"From Sluice."

"So where's your shirt? Never mind—I don't want to know."

He just shook his head, apparently forgoing any further questioning. He knew it wouldn't do any good. I headed for the shower and cleaned up, taking a little extra time with the shower gel and coconut shampoo. Slipping on Dan's NYPD T-shirt, I stuffed my dirty clothes in the laundry basket, thought about dropping my Doc Martens in a bucket of soapy water, but instead dropped them into the garbage can, and got myself a beer. Then I joined Dan on the couch.

"Mmmm, you smell nice now," Dan said, snuggling up.

"It's deodorant," I said, smiling.

"I love it." He snuggled closer, burying his face in my chest.

He proved it—at least until the light on my TTY began flashing half an hour later.

It was Del Rey Montez, my friend and the owner of the Memory Kingdom Mortuary. The message flashed in glowing red letters across the screen.

"BETTER GET OVER HERE, C.W. SLUICE'S TRAILER JUST BURNED TO THE GROUND!"

☞ CHAPTER XIII.

DAN AND I threw on our clothes and raced out of the diner. All I could think about was Sluice lying on the couch where I'd left him, semiconscious. I knew there was no way he could have escaped a fire in that trailer. Then I remembered the moving shadow that I'd thought was due to my overactive imagination. Maybe I really had seen something—or someone.

We hopped into Dan's Bronco and sped off toward town. By the time we arrived at the mortuary, the place seemed ablaze with patrol car, fire truck, and ambulance lights. A couple of kids standing nearby held their ears at what must have been fairly intense noise. The sirens didn't bother me, of course, although I could hear them slightly.

I pushed my way through the gathering crowd—nobody misses anything in Flat Skunk, even in the middle of the night—and headed for the cemetery. The fire was out by the time Dan and I reached the trailer, but the smell of burning wood, metal, and plastic lingered in the warm night air, competing with the scent of the towering pines. I spotted the sheriff talking with Del Rey, while his deputy was cordoning off the area around the trailer. I figured they could only do so much tonight. They'd be back in the morning when it was light again, to see what had caused the fire—carelessness on Sluice's part? Or arson?

Sluice was nowhere in sight. I ran to Sheriff Mercer, frantic with worry. "Sheriff! Sluice!" I puffed. "Is he—?"

Just then two paramedics appeared from the other side of the trailer, carrying a stretcher. Lying on the cot was the very still and nearly naked body of Sluice Jackson. Even his hemp necklace had been removed from around his neck. His skin was singed and red, but I couldn't tell the extent of his burns as the paramedics carried him by at a rapid pace. I followed him to the ambulance and teared up as I watched the EMTs hoist him into the ambulance.

My eyes were so blurred, I nearly missed what Sluice said to me just before they closed the ambulance door.

"...safe..." he said, then coughed violently.

"Yes, Sluice, you're safe." I blinked back the tears.

He coughed again. "No...no..."

But before he could say anything more, the door closed and the ambulance sped away.

I headed back to Sheriff Mercer and Del Rey, still huddled together. The sheriff was taking notes as Del Rey spoke, under one of the landscaping lights.

I couldn't help interrupting. "Is he going to be all right?"

The sheriff nodded. "Thanks to Del Rey, here. And her son, Andrew."

I looked around for Andrew and spotted him talking with Jeremiah Mercer and a couple of other friends. They were grinning and high-fiving him.

"What happened?" I asked Del Rey.

"Andrew thought he heard a noise outside his window, when he got up to use the bathroom. When he looked out, he saw smoke coming from the cemetery, then noticed the trailer was in flames. He yelled at me to call 911, then ran out to the shed, grabbed an ax and some gloves, and headed for the trailer. He chopped open the door, saw Sluice passed out on the couch, ran in through the fire, and dragged him out."

"Wow, that's incredible." I took a breath and collected myself, then shook my head remembering the last time I'd seen Sluice. "If only I hadn't left him...."

Sheriff Mercer looked at me. "What are you talking about?"

"I..."

"C.W.? Do you know something about this?"

"No, honestly, Sheriff. I just...I stopped by...earlier tonight. I wanted to talk to Sluice but he was drunk, lying on the floor. So I dragged him onto the couch...."

"You were here? What on earth for?"

"I...I just stopped by to ask Sluice a couple of questions. But like I said, he was passed out. He'd hit his head on the corner of his table. I washed off the blood—"

"He was bleeding?" The sheriff's eyebrows lifted another notch. "Why didn't you call an ambulance?"

"It was only superficial. Just a scratch, really. I figured he'd just sleep it off and I could talk to him in the morning. I had no idea—"

"Was he smoking one of his cigars?"

"No. Like I said, he was passed out. He wasn't doing anything but puking a little."

Del Rey grimaced when I said "puke." Sheriff Mercer looked disgusted, too, but I was sure it had to do with me, not the puke.

"Why is it, when something happens around here, C.W., you're not far away? Now why is that?"

"Sheriff, I had nothing to do with this! Maybe I shouldn't have left him alone, but..."

"It wouldn't have mattered," Del Rey said. "Sluice goes to bed drunk most every night. It's just lucky that Andrew heard a noise and woke up."

"Yeah, about that noise…" I said to Del Rey.

"What? Don't tell me you're hearing noises now, too? I thought you were deaf," the sheriff said.

"Funny," I snapped. "No, but I saw something—a shadow moving in the trees over there—when I came by earlier."

Sheriff Mercer looked at Del Rey, then back at me.

"You mean like a ghost or something?" He tried to suppress a grin.

"No. I don't know what it was. Just a dark shadow. That's why it's called a shadow, you know. 'Cause it's not real clear."

Sheriff Mercer squinted his eyes. He was either trying to visualize my mysterious shadow, or he was trying to come up with more questions for which I had no answers.

Dan appeared suddenly from behind the burned-out trailer. His hands were black from soot. "Sheriff, I found something. Just outside the trailer. You'll want to come take a look."

The three of us followed Dan as he moved around the burned wreckage of the trailer. It was only a smoldering shell now, a dark, smoky skeleton that had nearly become Sluice's funeral pyre. Sheriff Mercer gestured for Del Rey and me to stay back while he and Dan moved in closer. Dan pointed to the interior and said something I couldn't make out. I stared into the sooty darkness as they shone their lights but saw nothing except blackened refuse. Most of Sluice's meager possessions were burned to ash.

Dan moved his flashlight beam along what would have been the floor and held it at the center, where there was a large, gaping hole. He moved the light to what looked like a small trough made in the ash, as if something had been dragged through it. The light beam followed the rutted path to some weeds several feet beyond the trailer, where it seemed to end. Both men knelt down and pointed their flashlights into the trampled brush.

I sneaked up behind them and peered into the weeds to catch a glimpse of what Dan had found.

Something shiny winked back in the beam of the flashlight.

—·—

"What is it?" I said, too curious to hold back any longer.

Sheriff Mercer was too distracted by his find to care that I was there. I aimed my own flashlight toward his face so I could read his lips. "Looks like a metal box of some kind," he said, examining it only with his light beam.

"Looks like a small safe," Dan added.

Safe.

Sluice had said that to me when he passed by on the stretcher. I thought he meant he was "safe," as in "all right," but then he'd said, "No."

Was he talking about his safe?

Because he knew someone was after it?

"I think it's Sluice's safe," I said, kneeling down. I reached for it, but Sheriff Mercer grabbed my wrist.

"Don't touch it. Someone dragged this out here. If it wasn't Sluice, we'll need to dust for prints."

I nodded. I was dying to see what was inside. "This must have been what he was after," I said to myself. Apparently, I said it aloud because the hearing people nearby looked at me questioningly.

"Who? Sluice?" Sheriff Mercer asked.

"What do you mean, 'he'?" Dan asked.

"The shadow," I said, shrugging. It was all I had.

But this time Sheriff Mercer took me seriously. He frowned at Dan. "It does look like someone just dragged this thing out of

Sluice's trailer. The weeds are freshly trampled. Drag marks are pretty clear." The sheriff placed a finger on one corner of the safe and tapped it. "Still warm from the heat of the fire."

Dan stood up and peered into the darkness beyond the cemetery. I shone my light on his face. "Someone must have known that Sluice had this safe. Whoever it was entered the trailer, found Sluice passed out—or knocked him out, tried to find the safe, then set fire to the place. Maybe he wanted to get rid of Sluice. Or maybe he did it 'cause he knew the safe wouldn't be destroyed in the fire and that would make it easier to find."

"Or maybe both," I added. "But when do you figure he went in after the safe?"

No one said anything for a moment. Then Dan spoke up. "It looks like he did it sometime during the commotion to save Sluice and get him to the hospital. While we were all occupied with that, he must have come back, found the safe under the burned-out floorboards, and tried to haul it away."

"So it's likely that he suspected the safe was hidden in there," I added. It was common for miners to bury their loot under wooden floorboards in lieu of using the local banks. Sluice was old-school and more than likely would have distrusted the "newfangled" financial institutions.

Sheriff Mercer pulled some gloves from his back pocket and took hold of the safe at the bottom, trying not to touch more than he had to. I could tell the thing was heavy, but Sheriff Mercer was too macho to ask for help carrying it. Dan could have carried it with his pinky finger, but Sheriff Mercer continued to lug it toward the mortuary, puffing and sweating and probably cursing. I couldn't bear to watch his lips as he wheezed with the weight of the safe in his less-than-muscular arms. We followed him into the mortuary kitchen, where Del Rey was making coffee.

Del Rey threw a large dish towel on her kitchen table. "Set it here," she said. The sheriff hauled the safe on top, then stood back to admire the antique, as we all did. The faded words *Fargo Strongbox Company* were inscribed across the top of the black metal, in the curlicue letters that were popular in the 1800s. More curly designs decorated the top and sides, and the corners were covered in a silvery-looking metal. I had a feeling the safe itself would be worth several thousand dollars on "Antiques Roadshow." Sluice must have had the thing for years.

"Are you going to open it?" I had to know what was so important inside that safe that someone would try to kill Sluice and burn down his home. The sheriff ignored me. Instead he called out the door to his deputy, who waved away the few onlookers who hadn't gone back to their homes and their beds. Deputy Marca Clemens appeared in a few minutes with a fingerprint kit. The sheriff instructed her to dust the strongbox, lift the prints, and seal away the evidence in plastic bags. The whole procedure took less than fifteen minutes.

"That's it," Deputy Clemens announced officially.

I looked at the sheriff, almost drooling with anticipation.

He fumbled with the rusty lock, tried a few skeleton keys he had with him, then picked at it with one of Del Rey's turkey skewers. The lock refused to budge. Del Rey came at it with a small blowtorch she used for glazing the tops of crème brulées. Nothing. Andrew tried to knock the lock off with a bone-crushing hammer used in the cremation room. Nope.

Finally, I stepped forward. "Too bad we don't have the key," I said.

Sheriff Mercer looked at me like I was an idiot.

I continued. "Sluice always wore a hemp necklace with a key around his neck. I'll bet the paramedics took it off while they were working on him. Anyone know where they might have put it?"

Del Rey blinked. "As a matter of fact, they handed me a small plastic bag with a few personal items they found on him. I barely glanced at it. I think there were a few coins, a couple of rings, maybe a necklace, I don't know…"

"Get it," the sheriff said firmly.

Del Rey glanced around. "I…I don't remember where…" She began feeling her pockets, then looked around the room in a panic. "I…I don't—"

"What's up?" Andrew stood in the doorway. I guessed he was finished being congratulated by his friends and was probably ready for his "Town Hero" newspaper article.

"Andrew!" Del Rey said. "The paramedics gave me a small bag with Sluice's things inside. Do you happen—"

"You mean this?" he said, pulling the bag from his jeans pocket. "You handed it to me, remember? I was just about to give it to the sheriff." He turned toward Sheriff Mercer and held out the bag. "Here."

We all watched as Sheriff Mercer took the plastic bag from Andrew's hand and dumped the contents on the table next to the safe.

There it was. Attached to the hemp necklace. A key.

☞ CHAPTER XIV.

THE SHERIFF gave me a dirty look and gestured at all the tools on the table. "You couldn't have thought of the key before?"

"Sorry," I snapped. "I guess I was too busy worrying about Sluice to think about the key to his safe."

Sheriff Mercer stuck the key in the lock and in seconds the safe was open. He carefully pulled out the contents and set them on the table, as if they might be priceless artifacts. All I saw were old newspaper articles, more photographs of the relatives, a dried-up flower corsage, an old watch where time stood still, several birth, marriage, and death certificates, and a piece of an old flour sack.

That was it. No gold. No hidden nuggets or jewels or ancient scrolls or Lost Arks. Nothing of any value—except to Sluice.

Then why had the shadow been after the contents? Maybe he thought there was something valuable in there, just like we had.

"Not much here. But I'd better take a picture of it, in case we need to document it. Deputy?"

Deputy Clemens pulled a Polaroid camera from her evidence case and took pictures of each item. Then Sheriff Mercer was about to shove everything back inside the safe when I stopped him. "Wait. I think I'll take this stuff over to Sluice. I was going to see him at the hospital anyway, check on how he's doing. He might want these things with him. After all, he really seemed concerned about his safe."

"I doubt it. There's nothing much here. Best to put it all back where we found it and keep things safe for him."

I protested. "I know there's nothing of real value here, but they're his personal belongings and that's important to him. His last word to me was about his safe. I want to show him his stuff is still here."

Sheriff Mercer shrugged in grudging agreement. I asked Del Rey for a paper bag to carry the items, then Dan and I headed back to my diner to try to get a little more rest before dawn.

Ha.

———◆———

I dreamt I was being attacked by a dark shadow, then smothered, then set on fire, then doused with water. The water part turned out to be Casper, the Friendly Dog. He'd leapt up on the bed and was licking my face. At least it wasn't Dan licking me. He was still dead to the world, so to speak.

When I'd gathered my wits and roused a bit more, I wrestled with Casper until we annoyed Dan into wakefulness. He rolled over, his arm partially covering his eyes, and said something I couldn't make out. Rays of sun split through the blinds and I could already feel the rising heat of the day. Or was it the sight of Dan's steely bicep that was causing the temperature to rise?

"What the hell is going on?" Dan said. I could still barely read his lips under the crook of his arm.

I glanced at the clock. "It's time to wake up." My Shake-Awake alarm had apparently gone off but in my slumbering stupor, I had punched the "Off" button and slipped back to sleep. "Oh my God, it's after nine!"

I leapt out of bed and headed for the shower, while Dan threw mochas and bagels together for breakfast. I made a quick TTY call to Social Services, to find out Susie's status, and was told: No, Victoria Serpa wasn't in yet; no, there was no one there who could talk about Susie Littlefield's case; and no, they couldn't give out any information. Frustrated I hung up, finished my breakfast, and grabbed my backpack. We were out of there in less than thirty minutes, Dan to some kind of detective work and me to the hospital.

I made it just as visiting hours began. The volunteer at the front desk gave me directions to Sluice's room on the third floor. I headed up in the elevator with his bag of stuff from the safe in one hand and a copy of the *Eureka!* in the other, thinking he might like to read the story of his nugget find.

Sluice was sitting up in the hospital bed, mouth open and ready to catch flies, watching TV and playing with the remote. He didn't even glance at me as I entered the room.

"Sluice?" He finally took his eyes off the set. The last image I caught on the screen was Martha Stewart morphing into Jerry Springer.

Sluice closed his mouth and frowned at me, as if trying to place me.

"It's me, Connor." I held up the bag. "I brought you some of your things."

He continued to frown at me, then glanced back up at the TV. Just as Emeril was about to kick it up a notch, a black-and-white John Wayne rode into town on his horse. I took the remote from Sluice's hand, clicked off the TV, and set the bag on his bed.

"Sluice, you remember the fire last night?"

He blinked. He was looking pretty fuzzy.

"We found your safe. I brought you the contents."

Suddenly alert, Sluice grabbed the bag and dumped everything onto the bed. He dug through the mess until he found the scrap of flour sack. I would have gone for the photos or documents myself, but maybe this piece of trash had some sentimental value for him.

"Sluice, how are you doing?" Aside from the splotchy skin, which he'd already had anyway, he looked all right, for being old, alcoholic, and injured. His forehead was bandaged where he'd hit his head, as well as both his wrists and his chest. The rest of his body was covered with a hospital gown and sheet. Thank God.

He held the scrap out to me.

I took it and smiled. He was really out of it. Maybe they were giving him a little too much Demerol?

He tapped the scrap with his finger. "There it is. There it is," he repeated.

"Part of a flour sack. Yes," I said, almost as confused as he seemed to be.

He snatched the scrap out of my hand, turned it over, and handed it back. He tapped it again, more forcefully. "That's what they were after! My great-granddaddy's prop'ty."

I looked down at the material and noticed some writing on the back of the sack. The words were nearly unreadable, but drawn in a fine hand in the decorative, loopy scrawl of the past.

"What is it, Sluice?"

"That's my great-granddaddy's prop'ty. You go tell 'em!"

I had no idea what he was talking about. And I figured, neither did he. I was almost relieved when the nurse entered the room.

"What's going on in here?" she snapped. "He's not supposed to have visitors yet."

I hadn't noticed any sign on his door. Wouldn't have mattered either way.

"Sorry, I was just dropping off some of his things."

"You need to leave. Mr. Jackson needs rest. You can ask later to see if he can have visitors, but right now he needs quiet."

I wanted to say "quiet" was my middle name, but instead I set the piece of flour sack down on Sluice's bed. He lunged forward, snatched it up, and pressed it back into my hand, startling me.

"Show 'em," he said, looking pained. Maybe my coming to visit him wasn't such a good idea.

I nodded, hoping to calm him down, and he lay back against the pillow, closing his eyes. The nurse waved her hand toward the door. I took my exit—and the scrap of flour sack with me. My questions for Sluice about seeing Gail before her death would have to wait until Nurse Ratched was off duty.

———◆———

By the time I got back to town, I could hardly drive down the street for all the gold-seeking tourists. I was amazed at the far-reaching effect my little newspaper had—until I stopped at the newsstand to check out the competition. Chester had apparently given an "exclusive" to every paper in Northern California. Even the *Sacramento Bee* had the story—under the fold. No wonder the town looked like Mardi Gras on Bourbon Street. Only instead of getting drunk on Hurricanes, these tourists were high on the prospect of getting rich.

"Good God!" I said to Dan when I found him in his office. "The town's gone mad!"

Dan had his feet up on his desk, leaning back in his chair. Two electric fans were blowing warm air at him from two directions. I turned one of them my way and let the breeze blow over my sweaty arms and neck.

"Did you see Sluice?" he asked, pulling his legs from his desk to sit up.

"Sort of." I lifted my arm up so the air could circulate through my T-shirt. "He's kind of out of it, even more than usual. I brought him the stuff from his safe, but all he seemed to care about was this little piece of flour sack." I pulled the scrap from my pocket and held it out to Dan. "There's something written on the back that Sluice was rambling on about, but I can't make anything out."

Dan flipped the scrap over and squinted at the writing on the back. He got out his trusty detective tool—a magnifying glass—and held it over the scrap of cloth.

I caught only a few words as he struggled to read the script. "...property...to William Richard Jackson...signed Orville Orland...deeded this day, eighteen-something..."

Dan looked up. "It looks like a handwritten copy of a deed. It's incomplete, of course, and certainly not official. But the language is similar to deeds of the past. What's it supposed to mean?"

"Don't know. Does Sluice think his great-grandfather actually owned the Orland property?"

"If he does, this isn't going to do anything toward proving it. It's just a handwritten scrap."

"But what if it's legal? Can we somehow get it authenticated for him?"

Dan shrugged. "I could call around and see who does this sort of thing. But I doubt it's worth the paper—or cloth—it's written on. But if it *is* Sluice's property—and there's gold up there—he could end up a very rich man."

"And Chester Orland a very unhappy man," I added.

"Well, don't get your hopes up. It's going to take more than a few words on a flour sack to get Sluice his property—if it's rightfully his."

I went to my office while Dan made some calls. There were forty-seven messages waiting for me on my machine, but I wouldn't be able to take them until Miah arrived to translate. I figured I knew what they were anyway—questions about the article. With a story like this, everyone wanted to know more. My first call was to Social Services to check on Susie. My answer again was: No, Victoria Serpa was out on a call and wouldn't be back until later. No, they had no further information on Susie Littlefield.

And yes, they did have enough red tape, thank you very much.

"What's up, Connor?" Miah signed, as he burst through the door. "Hella hot already. I don't think I can work under these conditions." He plopped into his chair and switched on his computer. "What do you say we head for Lake Miwok and chill?"

"What do you say we put out an extra edition of the paper and make some more money?" I countered. "We've got big news here in little Flat Skunk and we have to take advantage of it. Starting with your friend's rescue last night."

"You corporate types. All that matters to you is the bottom line," Miah teased. "Cop dem," he said without signing.

"Cop dem?"

"Carpe diem," he repeated, overenunciating the words like an ape making faces at the zoo. Then he spelled the letters, which came out something like "Carp Deem." Miah was a phonetic speller.

"Oh, seize the day, eh? Well, how about you seize the messages on the machine while I seize the TTY and find out how your dad is doing with Josh."

While Miah took down the messages, I called Sheriff Mercer to find out if Josh's attorney had come by. Dispatcher Rebecca Mathews answered the call—I could tell by the way she typed. No punctuation and no TTY code. "SHERIFFS OFFICE HOW CAN I HELP YOU"

Rebecca knew it was me—I was the only one who ever used the TTY. Still I played the game. "Hi Rebecca, it's Connor. Is the sheriff there? GA."

"NO CONNOR HE GOT AN EMERGENCY CALL FROM CHESTER ORLAND AND TOOK OFF CAN I BE OF SERVICE"

"What kind of emergency call? GA"

"SORRY ITS A POLICE MATTER ILL TELL HIM YOU CALLED"

I gave up and hung up. A police matter involving Chester Orland. What now? Only one way to find out.

"Miah, I'll be up at Buzzard Hill if you need me. Tell Dan when he gets off the phone, will you?"

"What's up? Did they find more gold?" Miah asked.

I thought of Sluice and the remote possibility that he might own the land up there. "I hope so," I said.

I hoped that was all they found.

☞ CHAPTER XV.

I WAS PUFFING by the time I ran up to the crest of Buzzard Hill. Motor homes, SUVs, and small trucks clogged the two-lane road, causing drivers to slalom through what was left of the street. The place was crawling with mining poseurs, all standing around looking like they had no clue what they should be doing. Most, I expect, just hoped to stumble upon a large nugget and call it a day. Half these people would be gone for good by nightfall.

Sheriff Mercer was nowhere to be found. Had I misunderstood the dispatcher? She'd said the sheriff had received a call from Chester Orland and I'd assumed it had something to do with the find on his property. If it was his property. I asked a few tourists dressed in shiny off-brand jeans and sequined plaid shirts—apparently the latest in mining outfits—if they had seen or heard anything regarding the sheriff, but either they were too preoccupied with the possibility of becoming instant millionaires to notice, or the sheriff hadn't been here at all. Conspicuously absent were the Gold-digging Twins.

I spent a few more minutes searching the area. It wasn't easy with all those bodies in the way. Live ones, of course, all carrying dangerous weapons, like picks and shovels and heavy pans. I tripped over a rock the size of a soccer ball and thought about Gail. The sheriff said her head had been bashed in by a large rock. My mind drifted to Josh. There was no way he could have done something like that. Buzzard Hill was a waste of time. I had to see Josh.

The sheriff still wasn't in when I entered his office. Rebecca was busy taking a call, so I used the opportunity to sneak back to the jail cells and check on Josh.

"Hey, Connor," Josh signed, sitting up on his cot. Even lying down, he must have caught sight of the door. Deaf people are very visually aware. Almost any movement within the periphery of our vision catches our attention and alerts us to things that hearing people might miss. Like me, I had a feeling he'd see a pin drop from fifty feet away.

"Hi, Josh. How are you doing?" I signed back.

He stood up, tucking his rumpled shirt into his jeans, and moved closer to the bars. "All right," he said. As he grasped the bars, I could see his nails were bitten to the quick.

"Have you heard from your lawyer?"

Josh shook his head. "Nothing yet. He's supposed to be here any time. I wish he'd hurry." He tightened his grip on the bars again until his knuckles turned white and tried to shake them. Then he suddenly let go and banged the bars with open hands. "I'm going nuts in here, worrying about Susie. Have you seen her?"

The outburst startled me, but I empathized with his frustration. I'd tried to find out about Susie, I told myself, but not hard enough to assuage my guilt. I'd just been too distracted by Sluice and the fire.

"I've called a couple of times but I'm getting the runaround. I'll try again this afternoon, I promise."

Josh sighed and relaxed his hold on the bars.

"Josh, I had a thought. Someone said Gail was in the Nugget Café with you the night before she died."

Josh nodded. "We went for ice cream. But we had a fight, then Susie and I left."

"What was the fight about?"

"You know, the implant. Gail was convinced Susie had to have it and I refused to give my permission. She was furious at me, started swearing, so I took Susie and we went back to the bed-and-breakfast. Gail didn't come back for a while, so I let Susie sleep on a rollaway in my room. I guess Gail stayed at that diner to cool down."

I tried to imagine what was going on in Gail's head. What would I have done after an argument? Had a drink? Sat alone with my thoughts? Tried to come up with a way to convince Josh to change his mind?

I didn't like where that was leading me. If she'd returned to Josh's room, anything could have happened. He did have a temper—I'd just seen it. If she'd continued to provoke him…

I pushed that line of thinking from my head.

No, Josh wouldn't have killed her, no matter what. I had to believe that. After all, this was a man I'd once loved. And if I were honest with myself, I'd felt a flicker of that old flame recently. Had to push that away, too.

"Who else was at the diner, Josh?" I was hoping maybe someone else could tell me what Gail did after Josh left.

"It was late. Only a couple, three people. One crazy-looking old guy with a funny hat. Looked like he was talking to himself—his lips were moving, anyway, but there was no one with him. A couple of other guys at the back booth."

Sluice, mumbling to himself. Nothing unusual about that. "What did the other guys look like?"

PENNY WARNER

"Hell, Connor, I didn't pay attention," Josh signed fiercely. "I was dealing with Gail and her ranting." Josh shook his head and took a breath, as if calming himself. "Let's see...regular guys, I guess. Drinking beer and talking. I remember they stopped when Gail got really upset and started signing like some wild woman...." Josh thought for a moment, then continued. "I do remember one of them had on a hat with some lettering. US something. Thought he might be with the government. But that's it."

USGS? Could it have been Mike Melvin, the geologist? Talking to whom? Chester? Could have been anyone, really.

"What happened after the argument?"

Josh took another deep breath, this time as if he were bored with the question he'd soon be answering again and again. "I took Susie and we left Gail there. We went back to the inn. I got Susie ready for bed, asked the owner for a cot, and put her down in my room. Then I just waited for Gail to get back. Guess I fell asleep, 'cause I never saw her come in. I knocked on the door the next morning but didn't get an answer. So I got Susie dressed and we went to the reservoir."

"You didn't see Gail at all?"

"Actually, I never saw Gail again."

So, I wondered, what had happened after they'd had that fight at the diner?

"Josh, I'm going to see what I can find out about what Gail might have done after you left her. I'll check back this afternoon and see what your lawyer's going to do for you, okay?"

Josh nodded glumly, then reached out and took my hand with both of his. I felt a tingle—but it may have been anxiety over his circumstances rather than anything else. I hoped that's all it was. I was about to pull away when Josh's gaze darted to something behind me. I spun around.

Sheriff Mercer and Dan Smith stood in the doorway. Sheriff

132

Mercer looked angry and started right in on me. But I wasn't watching his lips. I was frozen to the spot, trying to read Dan's expression. Aside from a tightly clenched jaw, his face was unreadable.

I jerked my hand out of Josh's grasp so fast, I nearly got a skin burn. I wiped my palm on my pants, as if trying to rid myself of the evidence, then tried to focus on what the sheriff was saying. Although I already knew the gist of it.

When he finally took a breath, I bowed my head and slunk out of the room, passing awkwardly between the two men. I could feel the heat of Dan's body as I brushed by and my skin prickled.

Sheriff Mercer locked up the jail room and tossed the keys on his desk, giving Rebecca an angry look. She shrugged it off and went back to painting her pots. He didn't say anything for a few minutes, and neither did Dan, who was watching every move I made. I couldn't stand it any longer.

"I'm sorry, Sheriff! But you weren't here and I was worried about Josh. His lawyer hasn't shown up yet and he's scared, as you can imagine."

"It's not your business, C.W. You crossed the line by going in there without my permission. He's off limits from now on. Got it?"

I glanced at Dan but he'd stopped staring at me and was looking out a nearby window. Furious, I spun on my heel and slammed out of the office. They couldn't keep me from my next stop. I only hoped it held more answers than questions, because at this point, that's all I had.

—◆—

Mike Melvin and a couple of other geologists were housed in an old Whiskey Slide Victorian, converted into office space. I glanced at the sign nailed to the white clapboard exterior that announced UNITED STATES GEOLOGICAL SURVEY and headed up the front steps. The doormat, decorated with a large dog, read WELCOME ROCK HOUNDS. I knocked on the door, watching for shadows through the stained glass peek-a-boo window, then entered.

A government-issue secretary greeted me in the front room that was once a parlor. A couple of indestructible chairs sat along one wall, facing some geological-type sculptures mounted on wooden stands. In one corner a mining pan had been placed on a small table and filled with iron pyrite nuggets. Huge topographical maps of the area covered two of the walls. There was no mistaking the place for a dentist's office or hair salon.

The middle-aged woman looked up from her word processing and forced a fake smile. "Can I help you?" she said, without taking her hands from the keyboard.

"I'd like to see Mike Melvin. My name is Connor Westphal. I'm from the *Eureka!* newspaper."

I add the newspaper credentials when I think it will help. It's amazing how easily doors open when you're from the press.

"Oh! Do you have an appointment?" She stopped her typing and glanced over at her appointment book.

"No, I was just hoping to catch him. I have a few questions for an article I'm doing for the paper." It might be true. Someday.

"Well, I'll have to check. Do you want to take a seat?" She lifted her phone and dialed three numbers. I wandered toward one of the maps while she talked, then picked up a couple of fake nuggets and looked them over. When I turned back to see if she'd finished her conversation, she was staring at me strangely. I knew that stare.

"I'm sorry. I didn't hear you. What did you say?" It was obvious she had said something to me when my back was turned.

"You can go right in." She pointed to a door on the left. The name plate read MICHAEL MELVIN. I thanked her. She nodded, still looking at me strangely as I headed inside Mike's office.

The tall, fair man on the other side of a large oak desk stood and reached out a hand. He had a strong grip and a vigorous handshake. As a geologist, he probably stayed in pretty good shape with all that rock gathering and stuff. His light hair was almost transparent, cut short and combed straight up at the front. I took him to be in his thirties but it was hard to tell with his youthful face and hairstyle.

"Connor Westphal. I don't think I've had the pleasure. Although I've certainly seen your byline in the *Eureka!*. Read it every chance I get."

Yeah, sure, I thought. "That's great," I said.

"What can I do for you?" He sat down and gestured for me to sit in the chair opposite him.

"I had some questions about the recent gold discovery—for my newspaper—and I wondered if you could answer them for me and my readers. Just routine for you, I'm sure, but fascinating for us lay people."

"Be happy to. Fire away."

I asked some basic questions about gold and the likelihood that more nuggets would be discovered in the area. I took a few notes, most of them related to my "To-do" list and grocery needs. Good thing no one can read my handwriting. Under the guise of wrapping up, I closed my notebook and tried to sound casual with my next question.

"By any chance were you in the Nugget Café last night? This little girl I know saw someone wearing a hat with the letters USGS on it and really wants one. She hopes to become a geologist someday." Where do I get this stuff?

Mike looked over at a large crystal on his desk, which he apparently used as a hat rack. There sat the USGS hat.

"Yeah, I was there with Chester and them. I think I know the kid you're talking about. Cute little girl. Deaf, like her parents."

I nodded. Deaf people could rarely come and go anonymously in a town like Flat Skunk. They'd always be noticed.

"So you saw her and her parents?"

"Oh yeah, sure, couldn't miss them. The man and his wife were signing up a storm on the other side of the diner."

Mike wiggled his fingers, aping the signs. It was one of the most irritating things about Hearies—the way they tried to mimic sign language, as if it's some kind of hocus-pocus.

Mike went on. "Looked like they were having an argument, but I don't read sign language, so I couldn't tell. Their faces didn't look too happy though. That was clear enough."

I leaned in conspiratorially. "What was going on? Any idea?"

"Naw. All I know is, he got up and left, took the little girl with him. The woman stayed there for a while and finished her drink or whatever. We didn't pay her much mind after that."

"You were there with Chester, huh? He must be pretty excited about that gold nugget discovery."

Mike shook his head. "God, he's making my life a living hell. Wants to get all kinds of documentation about that gold discovery. Thinks it's going be the biggest find since Sutter's Mill."

"Was Sluice Jackson there?"

"Yeah, he was there, drinking his beer. He didn't stay long either. Why are you asking about this?"

"You heard about the woman who was killed yesterday?"

Mike looked stunned and took in a sharp breath. "You mean, that was her? Wow. Do they know what happened? There wasn't much in the paper—no offense."

I smiled. I get that a lot. "I don't know yet, but I'm trying to find out the facts for the *Eureka!*. Thought you might have overheard something he said or maybe gestured, like a threat or something." I put "overheard" in quotes.

Mike laughed. "That's not likely. They were signing the

whole time and I never learned the language of the deaf-and-dumb."

I winced at the word "dumb." It was an old-fashioned phrase coined years ago when deaf people were thought incapable of speech. It had become a derogatory term, much like "deaf-mute" or "dummy." Today the simple term "deaf" is preferred. Some even use "Deaf" with a capital letter. Personally, I prefer "Connor."

"Did you notice when the woman left?"

Mike shook his head.

"Did anyone meet her there after her husband left?"

"No. Far as I know, she was there alone."

"What about Sluice? How long did he stay?"

Mike thought a moment. "I think he left right before she did, but I can't be sure. Like I said, I was listening to Chester rattle on about his get-rich plans. I wasn't paying much attention to the other customers."

"What about Jilda or Mama Cody? Were they around?"

"Mama Cody took our order and brought out our beers. After that she disappeared into the kitchen, to clean up, I guess."

I stood up. "Thanks for your time, Mike. I'll be in touch if I have any more questions."

Mike Melvin stood and shook my hand. This time it was sweaty, reminding me of the waiting heat outside of the air-conditioned office. "Does the little girl want a hat? I got lots of them. She can have this one. It's adjustable." He removed the hat from the large crystal.

"That's really nice of you. I'm sure she would love it." Now what was I going to do with a USGS hat, I wondered.

"You take care now," Mike said.

I left the building with little more than what I'd brought—more questions. And a hat.

☞ CHAPTER XVI.

I FOUND DAN in his office, talking on the phone. I sat down opposite him, tried to read his side of the conversation, got bored, and started playing with a pencil on his desk. By the time he'd hung up, I'd built a fort out of his tape dispenser, stapler, pens and pencils, paper clips, coffee mug, and Rolodex, all held together with little sticky notes.

"What are you doing?" he said, after hanging up.

"I was bored. You weren't paying any attention to me," I said casually.

"Does it always have to be the 'Connor Show'?"

"Duh," I said, and topped the construction off with a fake nugget I'd lifted from the geologist's office.

"Where'd you get that?" Dan picked it up and examined it.

"Found it. Out in my backyard. Place is crawling with nuggets."

"Dog nuggets, you mean." He dropped the rock onto the desk.

I snatched it up. "Hey, that's gonna buy my way outta this little town," I said, quoting from some old movie.

Dan flipped the rock over with his finger. "Not with the letters USGS stamped on the bottom. Did you steal this from Mike Melvin's office?"

"I took it as evidence."

"Of what?"

"Of...his possible involvement in...whatever's going on around here."

Dan laughed.

"Seriously. He and Chester were at the Nugget Café the night before Gail was killed. They saw Josh and Gail arguing."

"So?"

"Well, so, nothing yet. But it could be important."

"So you stole his nugget. Do you make a habit of stealing men's nuggets?"

"I didn't steal it! They have them in the lobby as...favors, or whatever. And I resent the innuendo. You've still got your nuggets, haven't you?"

He reached down and grabbed his crotch.

"Stop that! God!"

He gave me an evil grin.

Before things went too far, I changed the subject. "So, have you heard anything about that skeleton from Arthurlene?"

"Yep. It's old, all right. Certainly could be Sluice's great-grandfather—or anyone else's for that matter. She's going to have a DNA test done to see if Sluice is really a descendant. That should settle it. But it'll take some time."

"What about that scrap of flour sack? What did you find out about the writing on the back?"

"It's over at Whiskey Slide. Got a handwriting specialist deciphering it. But even if it proves to be some sort of makeshift deed to the Buzzard Hill property, it's not going to be easy to prove. I doubt if it will hold up legally, especially after all this time. The Internet had some information on 'Squatter's Rights' that says something like, if you hold a property as your own for twenty years or so, you become the legal owner, whether you paid for it or not. That could be a problem, too."

I thought a moment. "Then why did someone try to burn down Sluice's trailer and get that safe?"

Dan frowned. "At least he's okay at the hospital, for the time being. Any idea when they're going to release him?"

"I don't know. I'm going over this afternoon to see if I can find out anything more about that night in the Nugget. I have a feeling something important went on there, and Sluice may know more than he thinks."

"Well, if Sluice knows, he may not be able to tell you. And if Josh knows, he may not choose to tell you."

At the mention of Josh's name, there was an awkward pause between Dan and me. It seemed to last an eternity. While Dan rapped on my office-supplies structure with a pencil, I could feel my heartbeat speeding up. Finally I couldn't stand it any longer.

"Look, Dan. I want you to know something. There's nothing going on between Josh and me—"

Dan held up a hand. "You don't have to explain anything, Connor."

"But I want to. When you walked in, I had just finished telling him how I was going to try to help him and Susie, and he was just showing his gratitude by clasping my hand. There was nothing more to it."

Dan nodded and said nothing, but he looked at me as if he didn't quite believe my words.

"He's an old friend, and I want to help him if I can. I know he didn't kill Gail. He's not capable of that."

Dan gave a half smile. "You'd be surprised at what people are capable of when the right button is pushed."

This time I looked at him, trying to read his meaning. I still couldn't.

I gave up and stood, slinging on my backpack. "I'm going to go back to the hospital and try to talk to Sluice. Why don't we meet for dinner at my place? I'll make your favorite—Hangtown Fry, Connor-style."

Dan nodded, but it didn't seem like a commitment nod, more like a "we'll see" nod. Apparently I was on some kind of probation. It sucked.

"Okay, then, I'll see you later."

Dan gave me a Mona Lisa smile, then picked up the phone and started talking, turning away from me. I wondered who had called. For that matter, I wondered if anyone had really called at all. How would I know?

But one thing I did know for sure. Dan was hiding something—for the first time since we'd become a couple.

———◆———

After swinging by the hospital's trendy new café for a mocha to go, I headed for Sluice's room on the third floor. When I stepped out of the elevator, I noticed a gaggle of nurses gathered at the end of the hall.

Sluice's room was directly across from them.

I started sprinting, then bumped into a tray of food and nearly toppled it, just like some stupid comedy. But the orderly didn't think it was at all funny. Luckily I couldn't hear what he yelled at me. I was off and running again.

"What's wrong?" I said when I reached the nurses. "Is it Sluice Jackson? Is he...?"

I looked into six pairs of eyes and got nothing. The old blank stare. The we-can't-give-out-that-information deadpan, zombie look that nurses are so good at.

I darted into his room before they could stop me. Sluice was gone.

I spun around in a panic. I didn't really want to know what I suspected. "Where is Sluice Jackson? Where have you taken him?"

A heavyset nurse with a look of sympathy on her gentle face approached me and took my hand. Her touch gave me a chill.

"Are you a family member?"

"No. I mean yes. I'm all the family he's got. Please, what happened. Is he…?"

The nurse turned to the others but no one said anything. Finally she turned back to me. "I'd let you see him if I could, dear, but I'm afraid that's not possible."

My heart plunged. "What have you done with his…with him?" I was growing more frantic by the second. If any sick people in the adjoining rooms were trying to sleep, I had a feeling they were fully awake now.

"Calm down, dear. We haven't done anything with him."

I blinked back the tears that were forming and waited for her to continue. When she took too long, I said, "Damn it, tell me! Where's his body?"

"We have no idea, dear. But he's certainly not deceased. He's just disappeared."

—◆—

After I got over the relief at hearing Sluice was alive, I began to wonder if someone had taken him. This hospital wasn't nearly as safe as I'd assumed. But if he'd left on his own, which was possible, knowing Sluice, I had a hunch where I might find him.

The gutted trailer still smelled of burnt wood and metal when I arrived. I saw something moving inside the skeletal frame and moved forward cautiously. Sluice. He was walking in circles inside the burned-out trailer, scanning the ground. I hoped the fire marshal had already done his investigation because Sluice was definitely trampling all over the crime scene. No length of yellow police tape was going to keep him away from his search—for whatever it was he was looking for.

It wasn't going to keep me away either.

"Sluice!"

He startled when I called his name from the blackened door-frame. His rheumy eyes blazed for a moment, until he finally placed me. He still wore the bandages over his forehead and wrists but he was dressed in his grimy old overalls and plaid shirt. That couldn't be good for his burns.

"What are you doing out of the hospital? Everyone's frantic, looking for you!"

"I don't need no hospital. I'm fine." He twisted his wrists as if to prove the point. "Anyways, I gotta find something important." He resumed his pacing around the charred ruins.

"What are you looking for, Sluice? Maybe I can help." I needed to get him out of there and back to medical care, but I couldn't just take him. I'd have to convince him somehow.

"My safe. I need to find my safe."

I blinked. Had he forgotten? "But Sluice, I brought you everything that was in the safe, remember?"

"I need the safe. The safe. I need the safe." He kept chanting as he shuffled through the ash and debris. I didn't know what to make of it.

"Sluice, stop. Listen to me. I took everything out of your safe and brought it to you at the hospital, remember. You gave me the piece of flour sack with the writing on the back, and I passed it onto Dan. He's checking it out. Everything's—"

He looked me squarely in the eyes. "I need my safe." I had no doubt in my mind at that moment that the old miner knew exactly what he was talking about.

"You want your safe," I repeated.

He nodded, not taking his eyes off me.

"Okay, uh, it's at the mortuary. In Del Rey's kitchen. At least, that's where we opened it. It may still be there."

He nodded once and we headed for the funeral home. Sluice knocked on the door, leaving a sooty imprint of his knuckles. I reached for the handle and opened the door to let us in. Del Rey kept it open during the day to allow "loved ones" to enter.

Sluice followed me into the lobby, where I called out Del Rey's name and rang the bell sitting on the counter. No response. After a few moments I led Sluice behind a velvet curtain, down the hall to Del Rey's kitchen.

The safe still sat in the middle of her wooden kitchen table. The tools we'd used to try to open it were gone, and the door to the safe was ajar; there was nothing inside. Sluice pushed the door back as far as it would go. I expected him to take another look inside, just to make sure it was empty. Instead he got out a Swiss Army knife from his back pocket and began unscrewing the tiny screws that held the back plate to the door. After he had removed three screws, the plate slid open, revealing a folded sheet of paper.

Those old safe-makers were full of surprises.

Sluice carefully lifted out the paper and unfolded it, leaving dark smudges on the corners where he'd handled it. There was another dark stain on the paper that had bled through the folds, leaving four marks, one lighter than the next but all the same blotchy shape. Sluice read over the printed matter, then passed the note to me.

I don't know much about legal papers, but it sure looked like an official deed to the Buzzard Hill property to me. Signed over to William Richard Jackson by Orville Orland. Dated April 14, 1851. I had a feeling this was the real deal.

And the stain that had bled through the paper looked a lot like dried blood.

☞ CHAPTER XVII.

"WELL, THIS IS a whole lot more official than that scrap of flour sack," I said to Sluice. He held the paper close to his rheumy eyes, his face pinched as though he smelled a bad odor. His eyesight was fading along with his brain cells, but he acted like he knew the paper he held in his hands was important.

"Let's take it to Dan. He'll know what to do."

Sluice folded the paper twice, stuck it in the chest pocket of his overalls, and buttoned the pocket shut. He gave it a final pat and followed me to my car. The ride to Dan's office took only a few minutes. Sluice rode quietly—at least I couldn't hear him, even though his lips moved slightly during the ride.

I parked in the back of the building where tourists aren't allowed and headed for the outdoor staircase. Sluice followed me, hunched over and moving slowly. I tapped three times on Dan's door—my signal—then opened it.

Dan was nowhere in sight. Odd, the door unlocked like that. I called out, did a brief search, asked Cujo the cat where Dan might be, then gave up.

"Sluice, how about I take you to Phil's assay office? It's not exactly his territory, but since Dan's not here, maybe he can tell us what to do with the deed. I'll leave a note for Dan to meet us there when he gets back."

I searched for paper on his desk and found a sticky note with a doodle on it. No pens. He'd cleaned up the mess I'd made. I yanked at the top drawer where he kept pens, along with a jumble of other office supplies; it wouldn't give. Must be stuck on something shoved inside there, I thought, and yanked again. Broke a nail, bit the rest off, and spat it out.

Why was Dan's drawer locked for the first time ever? I didn't even think he had a key.

"Let's go, Sluice," I said, giving the desk drawer a last frown.

Sluice frowned, too, then nodded and mumbled something I couldn't make out. I took it to mean he agreed. He followed me down the stairs to the sidewalk and along to Phil's down the street. When I turned back to check on him, I caught him glancing from side to side, still covering his pocket with his hand. And mumbling, of course.

"Phil!" I called out a few seconds after entering the office. Sluice shuffled in behind me. "Phil, are you here?"

Phil appeared from a back room, his jeweler's loupe attached to his forehead like an offset third eye. He looked pissed off about something.

"I said I was coming! You didn't have to shout!" Goodness. He was pissed off at me!

"I didn't think you heard us come in...." I stammered. "I just wanted to let you know we were here...."

He pointed to something behind me. I turned to see a small bell attached to a thin wire that hung over the door.

"Oh." I nodded. "You have a bell. Sorry."

"What is it you want?" Phil said abruptly. I didn't know the man well, even though he'd been in Flat Skunk all his life, but he was never one for a friendly chat. He mostly kept to himself, especially since his wife had left him recently. Rumor had it she had run off with another man and had taken everything with her except the assay business. Now he seemed to spend all his time here, except for the occasional meal at the Nugget.

"We—Sluice and I—we were wondering if you knew anything about claims, deeds, things like that, you being an assayer and all. Thought maybe you could validate this paper Sluice found."

Phil frowned and set down the rock he'd been holding. "What paper?"

I signaled for Sluice to show Phil the deed. Sluice reverently took the paper from his pocket and handed it over, his hands trembling, probably more from drink than from nervousness.

Phil unfolded the paper and read it over, then covered one eye with the loupe and studied the words and letters close up. After two or three minutes, he looked up, removed the eyepiece, and handed the paper back to Sluice.

"Can't say for sure," he said. "Looks authentic, but you'd have to send it to Sacramento to get a legal confirmation. Not my area of expertise."

He turned around abruptly and went back into his workroom without another word. I wondered if his wife left him for being socially challenged and etiquette-impaired. Not even a "Thanks for stopping by."

"What now?" I asked Sluice, not expecting an answer. Even if I got one, I probably wouldn't be able to understand it. So I answered myself. "How about we go see the geologist? He might have old records of the land that could tell us something. And maybe there's someone on staff who could authenticate the deed." What did I know?

Sluice nodded, mumbled something, then headed for my car. As we rode down Highway 49 toward Whiskey Slide, Sluice stared out the window, resting his arm on top of the door. He seemed to be enjoying the wind as it lifted the sparse hairs on his head and grinned at me from time to time. In my Chevy with the top down, he looked almost like an aging rebel teen.

We let ourselves into the USGS office and waited for the secretary to alert Mike Melvin that we were there. Sluice ran his fingers through the bowl of fake nuggets, then tried to bite one, probably out of habit. I had to push his hand down before anyone saw him. Just then the secretary motioned us to go in. I took Sluice by the hand and led him into Mike's office.

"Connor! Good to see you again!" Mike said brightly. His lips were easy to read, at least compared to Sluice's. "What can I do for you this time? Need more information for your article?"

He had tried hard to ignore Sluice, as if the old man were a large ugly tumor attached to my hand. But I caught him stealing a glimpse and stifling a grimace. I pulled Sluice up beside me. "Thanks, Mike. I want you to meet Sluice Jackson, a friend of mine. We have a question for you."

Mike reached out to shake Sluice's hand, but Sluice just stood there. I had a feeling Mike was relieved to pull his hand back. He gestured toward a couple of chairs. "Have a seat."

We sat down and Mike followed suit, folding his hands on top of his desk indicating we had his undivided attention.

"Sluice, show him the paper."

Sluice slowly pulled the deed from his pocket and handed it to Mike. Mike read it over and looked up at me. "What is this?"

"We thought you might be able to tell us. Sluice has had it in his possession for years. He thinks it might be a deed to the Buzzard Hill property."

"You mean Chester Orland's land?" Mike seemed incredulous.

I nodded. "It looks like the property was signed over to William Richard Jackson by Orville Orland back in 1851. We want to know if it's legal. Because if it is, then Sluice could be the rightful owner of that property."

"Well, uh, I'd have to do some checking. Can you leave it with me for a few days? I'll have some of my people do the research."

"No!" Sluice shouted and snatched the paper out of Mike's hands.

"Sluice! That's rude. He's not going to keep it. He wants to check it out. That's what you want, remember?"

"It's mine! No one's takin' it from me." Sluice stood to go.

"Calm down, Sluice." I turned to Mike. "Could you make a photocopy of it for now? Then if you need the actual document, I'll make sure you get it."

Mike nodded. "I suppose we could do some checking with a copy, but I'll need the original to really authenticate it."

I turned to Sluice. "Let him make a copy of it. He'll give it right back."

Sluice reluctantly handed the paper over to Mike, but he followed him into the copy room, refusing to be separated from the deed. Mike seemed reluctantly tolerant of Sluice, much as a spinster aunt would behave toward a mentally disabled relative. Talking down to a disabled person and treating him like a child is a common reaction by people who don't understand handicaps. I had received similar treatment by hearing people at times. They treated me as if I were retarded, not deaf.

Mike handed over the original. Sluice folded it up and stuck it in his pocket. As Sluice headed for the door, I thanked Mike for his help. When I told him it was important, he promised to get back to me by the next morning. It was the best we could do at the moment, without Dan's help.

And where was Dan, anyway?

—◆—

By the end of the day I had finished most of my work for the newspaper, editing a special edition for the tourists who had flooded the area with picks and pans and paper money. I also wrote a piece on the mystery of Gail's death but didn't have a lot to add since little had been released from the coroner's office. And my heart wasn't in it. It had hit too close to home.

I hadn't gotten over to see Josh again; I figured he was off limits to me anyway. Nor had I called Social Services again to check up on Susie like I'd promised, but I'd felt overwhelmed with more pressing tasks and was tired of the runaround. Still, I managed to get Sluice checked in once again at the hospital—and formally released with a physician's approval. I left him at the mortuary where he was busily turning an old shed into a homestead, with Del Rey's permission. He saw it as only temporary, since he was certain he'd be inheriting the Buzzard Hill property any moment.

Dan had still not returned…and I was getting worried. It wasn't like him not to check in once in a while.

Around 6:00 P.M. my grumbling stomach reminded me it was time to eat. I put the newspaper to bed, sent Miah to the printer on his way home, and headed for my own home and an eclectic plate of refrigerator potpourri—a specialty of mine.

The mystery of Dan's whereabouts was cleared up by the time I got home. He was waiting on the front step when I drove up, petting Casper with one hand and holding a beer in the other.

"Where have you been all afternoon?" I asked, closing the car door and ambling over as though I didn't really care. He'd been acting odd ever since Josh had come to town, and while I wanted to reassure him there was nothing going on between Josh and me, I didn't want to make it too easy for him either. A man who was too comfortable was a man who took you for granted. At least that was true of my ex.

"Doing this and that," he said vaguely. Casper's jaw snapped twice, barking his own two cents. Neither statement was very clear.

"Hungry?" I said, stepping around him and unlocking the front door.

I had my back to him, so I didn't catch his response. I assumed he was. I knew Casper was hungry. I could see his tail wagging out of the corner of my eye. If Dan had had a tail, I'll bet it would have been wagging, too.

I invited the two of them in, then set down my backpack loaded with paperwork and other crap. I headed for the fridge and helped myself to a beer, then slid into a booth. Dan joined me, while Casper went for his bowl of dog chow du jour.

"Learn anything?" I asked, after a couple of swigs.

"This and that," he said again.

"What and what?" I asked. He wasn't going to get away with vague answers anymore.

"Well, the skeleton they found is more than likely over a hundred and fifty years old. DNA test results still won't be ready for a few days, but the forensic anthropologist could determine the age from a few chemical tests."

"So it could be Sluice's great-grandfather."

"It could be anyone's great-grandfather."

"Anything more on Josh's wife?" I took another swig to prepare myself for his answer. Although I hadn't known her well, the details of any death were disturbing.

"Yeah. She died from trauma to the head—probably a blow—sometime after midnight, then was put into the trunk of the car. No fingerprints, hairs, or anything found on or near her body. They did find an appointment card with the audiologist."

"Was the card significant?"

"Not in itself. But on the back she had written the letters 'USGS' with a question mark next to them."

"Why would she write that on the back of her audiologist's card?"

"Good question. Got any ideas?"

I thought a moment. The only thing that came to me was the possibility that she'd seen the hat logo in the Nugget Café, too. But why make a note of it?

"Well, you accomplished a lot, but you left your office door unlocked. I was kind of worried about you."

Dan frowned. "I did? No, I'm pretty sure I locked it. In fact, I know I did. I remembered I'd forgotten something and had to unlock the door, then I secured it again, thinking what a pain that was."

"Well, it was unlocked. Nothing disturbed as far as I could see. You may want to check. But a funny thing—your top desk drawer was locked. I didn't even know you had a key."

Dan nodded thoughtfully and I expected him to give me some kind of vague response. Instead, he switched the subject. "So what did you do this afternoon?"

I filled him in, which in retrospect seemed like very little. As I talked about my day, my frustration grew. I got up from the booth, opened the refrigerator, and stared inside, pondering the possibilities of combining cheddar cheese singles with blueberry yogurt, mixing in a shredded carrot, some chocolate sauce, and a hard-boiled egg. I about threw up into the refrigerator.

"How about a couple of pasties at the Nugget?" Dan asked, when I turned to him for help.

"Sounds divine."

We were in our favorite booth within twenty minutes, a couple of hot pasties on the way and two beers in front of us. Things just didn't get much better than this in Flat Skunk.

Sheriff Mercer and Deputy Clemens entered the café a few minutes later and sat in the booth next to us. As our food arrived,

Sheriff Mercer pulled out his cell phone and took a call. A minute later he stood up, slapped his phone shut, and said something to his deputy.

The hairs on the back of my neck stood up. I knew that look on his face. "What's wrong, Sheriff?"

"Can't talk right now, C.W. Got an emergency."

"What is it? What's happened?"

The sheriff gave me a hard look. "I don't know, C.W. Alls I know is, we got us another body up on Buzzard Hill."

"Another body? You mean another skeleton?"

The hairs all over my body stood at attention. I got up from the booth and followed the sheriff out the door. Dan caught up with us a few moments later. I hoped that meant he'd paid our bill.

We never did eat those pasties.

☞ CHAPTER XVIII.

IT WAS STILL light out and probably would be for another hour or two. The heat was starting to abate, but the pavement radiated enough warmth to cook up some Hangtown Fry. If I'd had the ingredients, which I didn't. Dan and I headed for my sweltering Chevy, while the sheriff got into his patrol car, lights blinking and sirens screaming. I could faintly hear the rhythmic pulse of the sirens. Sheriff Mercer pulled over at Buzzard Hill, jumped out, and started up the grade, with Dan and me right behind him. I saw Chester Orland, standing in front of the old Buzzard Mine with the Josephs and a number of miners around him. Today the couple were dressed in black cargo pants and matching black tank tops that each sported the word GOLD DIGGER in gold ink. Chester began waving his arms at the sheriff.

If Chester had found another skeleton, whose bones were these, I wondered, climbing the hill. Chester's ancestors? Not likely, since Chester had said his dead relatives were all buried in the old Pioneer Cemetery. Was it just a long-lost miner who'd had some bad luck? Or was Buzzard Hill some kind of prospectors' burial ground? They probably called it Buzzard Hill for a reason.

I was puffing when I caught up with the sheriff. He'd reached the mine entrance only a few seconds before me and he was more than puffing. He was gasping for breath. Guy needed to lose some weight and get more exercise. But he never would.

Between puffs I glanced down at the center of the circle formed by the onlookers. Someone had covered the bones with some kind of heavy-duty plastic bag. Sheriff Mercer looked at Chester for an explanation. Chester said nothing. Instead, he bent over and pulled back the top of the plastic.

This was no pile of old bones.

A fully fleshed-out body lay sprawled face down on the ground. The body of a man.

I felt sick as Sheriff Mercer knelt down and gently rolled the body over enough to expose the man's face. It was nothing more than a mass of pulp, completely unrecognizable. But from the lettered cap that sat askew on his bloody head and the government logo on the front of his jacket, the man's identity wasn't difficult to figure out.

USGS.

The dead man had to be Mike Melvin, the geologist.

I had just seen the man! I thought, suddenly shivering. He was a living, breathing human being. Now he was mangled flesh and blood.

"Back off, folks! Back off," Sheriff Mercer called to the crowd, who mostly stood wide-eyed, some with their hands covering their open mouths. Seconds later the sheriff was on his cell, calling for reinforcements. No doubt Arthurlene would also be notified. It was déjà vu all over again.

"Sheriff! You've got to do something!" Chester Orland began ranting. Spittle formed at his lips as he spoke. "We got a serial killer loose around here! First it was that deaf woman and now it's my buddy, Mike Melvin. What are you going to do about it, Sheriff?"

Sheriff Mercer ignored his comments. "Stand back," he repeated, waving his arms in an attempt to control the gawking, curious crowd. "Chester, get these people out of here. Now!"

The sheriff was no dummy. Put the agitator to work and keep him out of your hair while you do your own work. Chester loved to be in charge. He'd be great at getting everyone to retreat— including himself.

Within moments Deputy Marca Clemens and Dr. Arthurlene Jackson arrived with their various bags and cases full of official equipment. While Deputy Clemens helped with crowd control and evidence collection, Arthurlene put on her latex gloves and went to work on a preliminary exam of the body. It was pretty clear Mike Melvin had died of trauma to the face and head, but the deputy could find no sign of the weapon used to smash the man's skull in.

"Look here," Arthurlene finally said to the sheriff, after spending fifteen minutes or so examining the corpse. I'd been watching her like a hawk, eager to see what she found—if anything. She pointed to Mike's right hand, which was balled into a tight fist at his side.

"Rigor?" The sheriff asked, nodding at the stiffness of the limbs.

Arthurlene knelt down on one knee and inserted a pen into the crevice of the fist where the thumb and index finger curled together. With a strong twist, she turned the hand over.

There was something in Mike's hand.

The sheriff, Dan, and I all peered closer to see the object clutched in Mike's death grip. Arthurlene peeled back the index finger, then the middle finger. A small gold nugget rolled out from the dead man's grasp onto the dirt. Arthurlene picked it up with two gloved fingers.

Someone bumped my backside. I turned to see Chester straining his neck, trying to join the circle. "Is that a nugget? If it is, I know he found that on my property!" Chester said, looking almost frantic. "And if he did, it's mine, you know."

Dan shook his head in disgust. The others ignored Chester. But his words made me think. I stood up and glanced over at a sign I hadn't seen until now. Chester must have erected it just that day. It read, WELCOME TO THE BIGGEST GOLD RUSH SINCE SUTTER YELLED EUREKA!

I glanced back at Chester. He looked stricken. Was he genuinely concerned about Mike's death? Or was he worried about possibly losing his own life? Three bodies had been discovered in Flat Skunk in the past couple of days. One an antique, nothing but bones. One an out-of-town visitor, who wasn't here for the gold. And one involved because of his occupation.

Was there a connection? Or was it all random?

I thought about the fire at Sluice's trailer and the hidden deed. Were they connected? I didn't know how exactly, but I sensed Chester was somehow involved.

But Gail's death threw the whole theory off. What, if anything, was the connection there? The whole situation was making me sick.

———◆———

Soon after sunset the excitement died down, along with the temperature. Dan and I headed back to my diner for a cold beer and a cooling bath. I was covered with red dirt smudges that had mixed with sweat and turned to deep bronze. I needed to get out of my filthy clothes and into some clean water. Dan decided to join me.

While I ran a tub, Dan got the beers. I was already in and

covered with bubbles by the time he'd stripped out of his own dirty clothes. As he stood by the tub and handed me my beer, I got an eyeful before he stepped in. The water rose another couple of inches and a few bubbles sloshed over the side of the tub, but it was refreshing and relaxing, not to mention cozy.

After trying out some new hair styles on Dan's wet hair and covering his beard with bubbles, I settled into the tub to soak. The water temperature had turned tepid, which felt good against my warm skin after hours of baking in the summer heat. The conversation turned to events of the day.

"So what do you think is going on?" I asked Dan. He looked as if he were about to fall asleep in the bath. His head rested against the wall, and his arms on either side of the tub rim. I sat between his slightly bent legs and played with my new, somewhat buoyant, bath toy while I talked.

"I think it feels gooood," Dan said, without opening his eyes.

I squeezed my bath toy. "Not that! The body! Everything that's happened in the past couple of days."

Dan shrugged, but he still had that goofy smile on his face. I squeezed a little harder.

"Hey!" His eyes shot open as he flinched. "Cut it out!"

"Now that I have your attention, what do you think?"

Dan relaxed but kept his eyes open, probably watching for another attack. "I don't know what to think. Except that Chester seems to be worried he's going to be murdered by a serial killer—although I don't know why he would think that. There's no motive that I can see for whacking him. Except that he's annoying as hell."

"Whacking? What, is everyone in the Mob now?"

"I'm from New York. What can I say?"

"I guess you can say whacking. Then why was Mike whacked? There doesn't seem to be a motive for that either."

PENNY WARNER

"Maybe he knew something about the nugget Sluice found. Or the bones buried up there. And he had that nugget in his hand. Maybe he found gold and someone offed him for that."

"Why wouldn't they take the nugget that was in his hand then?"

"Good question," Dan said. His eyes started to glaze over again. I gave him a gentle reminder. His eyes blinked open. "All right, all right!"

"Let's look at the big picture," I said. "Maybe Mike found out that land had a hidden vein somewhere and wanted to check it out. Somebody else also knew about it and killed him to keep him from discovering it—or telling anyone if he did discover it. That could be Chester himself."

"Well, I've been doing a little investigating, while you've been flirting with Josh and playing nursemaid to Sluice."

"I was not—"

Dan held up his hand. "Just kidding."

I frowned but didn't have time to be angry. I wanted to know what he'd found out. "Well?"

"You know the couple who found the tooth—Jana and Tim Joseph? Turns out they're not just tourists. They're amateur archeologists but not exactly legitimate ones. Seems they have a reputation for joining archeological digs, pilfering the finds, and selling them on the black market. Like Forty-niner artifacts, old Levis, bones."

"You mean that old skeleton could be worth some money? Or do you think maybe they know something else is up there and they don't want anyone else finding out?"

"Possibly. Then there's Mike himself. Apparently the job at the USGS office in Whiskey Slide was a demotion. He used to work in Washington, but he allegedly falsified some documents for a payoff and got sent to Whiskey Siberia. They couldn't prove anything, but he's not looking good."

"Not now that rigor mortis has set in," I added. "How did you find all this out?"

Dan smiled. "And then there's Chester, the primary suspect in my book," he went on, ignoring my question. "He's been trying to make money off that property for years. I think he's been salting the mine and the area around it in order to raise interest and sell stock in the property. I think the nuggets are completely bogus."

"Good theory. But what about Gail? She seems to be a loose cannon." Gail. I still couldn't believe she was dead. I thought of poor Susie, now motherless. There is nothing more cruel, more painful, than losing your mother, especially so young. Except maybe losing your child.

"Maybe not. Maybe she overheard something between Chester and Mike that night."

Shit. Dan had been doing all the work I should have been doing as a news reporter. It was my job to dig up the dirt. Had I just been too distracted by Josh?

There were still some loose ends. "But why burn down Sluice's trailer, then? Just to get the safe? Someone must have known about the possibility of a deed hidden inside."

"You know Sluice. He's not always so good at curbing his tongue. Maybe he bragged about it and hinted where it was. Then again, maybe the killer wanted Sluice out of the picture for a different reason."

"Maybe. But the whole thing doesn't fit together. Something's missing."

I stood up and stepped out of the tub, dripping cold water on the linoleum floor.

"Where are you going?" Dan asked, sitting up, suddenly alert. "I wanted to talk to you about something."

I grabbed a towel, dried off, and started putting on fresh underwear, jeans, and a T-shirt. "I just had a thought," I said.

"What? Does it involve your new bath toy?"

I gave him a "get-real" look.

"Why are you putting on your clothes?"

"I have to make a quick trip to my office. I'll be right back."

"At this hour? Can't it wait? Your bath toy is starting to sink." Dan nodded toward the water.

I stifled a laugh. "Sorry, but this is more important than your SOS. Try to stay afloat until I get back."

"Enough with the ship metaphors. What's up?"

I smiled. I could just see the crow's nest peeking out from under the dissipated bubbles. The ship hadn't completely sunk.

"When I get back, any chance you could be wearing an eye patch or something?" I winked at him.

"Aye, matey. You plan to do some pillaging?"

"That depends. You got some gold coins for me?"

"Something better than that, I hope," Dan said. "Shiver me timbers."

"I plan to," I said, and grinned all the way to my car.

☞ Chapter xix.

WHEN I WATCH a horror movie, I can always sense when something scary is about to happen. Unfortunately, I had no impending sense like that as I walked up the semi-dark staircase to my office. There were still a few tourists strolling the streets and plenty of lights coming from a few still-open shops. I felt completely safe, even after the discovery of Mike Melvin's murder. In spite of all the bodies, Flat Skunk is one of the safest places to live. Of course, that could all change if they didn't stop turning up.

The light in the hallway blinked intermittently, a sign of old and faulty wiring that probably hadn't been brought up to code since the Penzance Hotel was converted into shops and offices over fifty years ago. I sometimes worried about the possibility of a fire—it was especially on my mind with Sluice's recent burnout—but since I rely heavily on my sense of smell, I figured I'd get a whiff of smoke in time to get out of the building. Hell, my sense of smell is so good, I can usually tell what Dan has had for lunch, when Rebecca Mathews has sneaked a joint, and when Sheriff Mercer has spent some time with his perfumed lady friend, Sheriff Peyton Locke.

I stuck my key in the office door lock and jiggled it around.

The door didn't open. I tried pulling the key out, but it appeared to be stuck. After more jiggling, a little cursing, and a brief tantrum, I managed to break the key off in my hand.

Now what? I thought, staring at the doorknob as if waiting for a genie to appear and solve my problem. I pulled out a paper clip from my backpack, got down on my knees, and stuck the paper clip into the lock, easing it in next to the broken key part. After more creative jiggling, the paper clip slid in deeper. I felt a click. The door opened.

I could be a burglar, I thought, if this newspaper gig doesn't work out. I was feeling pretty cocky as I entered my office and switched on the light. I glanced around the room, took in a deep breath of air, then coughed. It wasn't smoke I smelled, but there was definitely a new odor in the room. Cleaning fluid? The janitor must have already been there.

I checked the wastebasket. Full to the brim, mostly with discarded paper. There might have been a whole tree inside that basket, I thought, feeling a twinge of guilt. The janitor must have missed it. I sniffed a few times and still couldn't place the smell beyond something having to do with cleaning products. Didn't matter. The odor would be gone by morning.

I headed for my filing cabinet and pulled open a drawer. It had taken some coaxing, but I had finally convinced Sluice that someone might be after his deed and that it would be safer with me. Then I had cleverly hidden it among a bunch of other papers in the file marked CRAP. No one looking for something important would ever look in a file called CRAP.

I pulled out the file and riffled through it. The deed was hidden among other important papers, like recipes I would never try, vacation spots I'd never visit, and other careers I'd never take on. I found the recipe for Death by Chocolate, the brochure for the Smithsonian, and the job description for Police Cadet.

The deed, however, was gone.

I checked through two more times just to make sure. Someone had definitely been in my files and had taken the deed I had been guarding for Sluice. He wasn't going to be happy with me.

But I didn't have time to worry about that. I suddenly got a strong whiff of something chemical-smelling. The odor was bitter, almost burning. I whirled around to see a dark figure wearing a silly frog mask.

"Dan! You scared me! Don't tell me you want frog sex—"

The giant frog grabbed my hair. He pulled me over backwards, causing a painful snap in my back, and shoved a putrid rag over my nose and mouth.

I kicked and scratched and shook my head and tried to bite the hand holding the rag, but in my awkward position I had no leverage. I kicked the air a few more times and swung my arms wildly.

And then, right before the room went completely black, I just didn't care about anything anymore.

<hr />

Hangover?

That was my first thought. Dry mouth, body aches, no idea where I was. I hadn't been this hung-over since college. I thought about lifting my head but it throbbed too much. I wanted to go back to sleep, but something told me I wasn't in my lumpy fold-out sofabed. Granted this bed was lumpy, but it was also cramped, cold, and smelled like…what?

The smell at my office came wafting back. Chemical. Mixed with something else. Plastic?

My head shot up and hit a soft restraint. I was fully awake, my eyes were open—at least I thought they were—but I couldn't see anything but blackness.

This was no hangover.

I tried to move my arms. One arm had no feeling. It lay under my stomach. The other ached too much to move.

I tried to roll over, but when I moved my legs, both throbbing in pain, I found them trapped inside a kind of plastic wrap. I forced my dead arm out from under my stomach and tried to push myself up using my elbow, but the plastic casing limited my movements.

I reacted without thinking, batting at the body bag—or whatever it was—with my legs and one arm, but it held tight. I kicked at it repeatedly, wasting my energy, strength, and breath.

Calm down, Connor, I said to myself. Think. It's only plastic, it's not steel. You can get out of this. Think. Before you use up all your air and suffocate in this giant garbage bag.

I mentally pictured my pockets. A few coins. A couple of Hershey's Kisses for makeshift mochas. My keys.

My keys.

My dead arm was coming back to life and now prickled with pins-and-needles after being deprived of blood for who knew how long. My other arm, the one that ached, was almost completely useless. I forced my prickling arm into my pocket, hooked the key ring with my finger, and slid the keys out. Feeling for the right key, I scraped my finger on the edge of the one I'd broken off in my office lock.

It would be perfect.

I held the jagged edge of the key up to the plastic barrier, shoved the plastic taut between my knees, and began scraping at it repeatedly. I had only one thought as I worked the key into the plastic—I would eventually run out of air if I didn't make a tear soon.

The prickling in my arm disappeared, only to be replaced by more aches and pains, but I kept at it, promising myself a hot tub and some soothing body lotion after all this was over. While I worked, I had time to think about how I'd ended up here. It came back to me in broken pieces, like parts of a dream, a nightmare that doesn't connect.

I had been at home…I remembered being with Dan in the tub. But I left and went to my office…to get, what?…Sluice's deed! The key had broken off in the lock…I used a paper clip…the room smelled funny, a chemical smell, like cleaning products. I went to the cabinet…pulled out the file…it was gone! Sluice's deed had been stolen.

And then…something about a giant frog…

I shoved the key fiercely into the plastic, angry at what had happened. The jagged edge pierced through unexpectedly. In the follow-through, my hand hit hard against a rough surface at my side. Sticking my finger through the small tear, I poked and pulled, enlarging the hole enough to squeeze my hand through. Using my foot as leverage, I continued pulling and tugging at the hole until I could finally get my legs out.

Moments later I was out of the bag.

It was still dark, but now I could move more freely, within limits. As I felt around with my useful arm, I realized how confined I really was. The space was hardly larger than my supine body. It was cramped, cold, damp, and smelled of decay.

I had a good idea where I was.

A mine shaft.

Whoever had attacked me had wrapped me in some kind of plastic bag and thrown me into a mine shaft. That's why I had all those aches and pains. It's a wonder I didn't have a crushed skull. I had no idea how far I'd fallen, but I'd been lucky enough not to fall right on my head. It felt like my arm had taken the brunt of it, while my head had landed on something softer than the hard ground.

I felt the floor around me. Dirt and rock and something soft under where my stomach had lain. More plastic?

I moved my hand farther up, where my head had landed, and touched a solid but pliable mound, also covered in the same plastic material. It gave as I pressed on it. Whatever it was had kept my head from cracking open upon impact and for that I was grateful. If—or when—I got I out of here, I'd take the damn thing with me and mount it with some kind of plaque. "This object saved the life of Connor Westphal, nosy reporter...."

I felt along the base of the mound to see how big it was—and whether it was something I could use to get myself out of this pit. My hand traveled up a few inches of the solid mass and I felt the form within.

My hand jerked back. There was something inside. Warm, but not moving. Instinctively I recoiled as far as I could from the thing but managed only a few inches before I hit the wall of the tiny mine shaft.

Someone—or something—was in there. And it could also still be alive. If it was a human being, I had to get the plastic open. If it was an animal...I had to find out.

I poked a finger at it, hoping that would tell me everything I needed to know. It didn't. I opened my hand and patted the thing, trying to get an outline of it without taking in too much sensory information. At the top I found a drawstring, tied tightly. There wouldn't be much air inside the bag with the end so securely tied. As much as I dreaded the prospect, I had to get the bag open before it was too late.

If it wasn't already.

In the darkness, I dug at the string with my nails until I had one part loosened. I pulled at it with my teeth until it finally gave. With one good arm and one leg, I stretched open the top.

The smell of rotting decay hit me like a blast. I almost threw up. After regaining my composure, I reached in and placed my hand on something furry.

An animal?

What could it be? Had I been tossed in here with a bear, or a mountain lion, or a wolf? I patted the fur again, slowly, as lightly as I could, moving downward. And then I felt something wet and hard.

Teeth.

I was about to pull my hand away when the damn thing bit me.

"Ouch!" I cried. Whatever it was, it was alive. I pulled back against the wall as far as I could, trying to escape the hairy beast. I had no idea what I was up against, trapped inside that deep, black pit.

But I could sense it was coming closer.

The stench was growing stronger.

☞ CHAPTER XX.

IN THE DARKNESS, the figure grabbed me around the waist. I screamed again, then took in a sharp gasp of air so I could keep screaming until someone heard me—or until I could no longer scream anymore.

It was that gasp of air that stopped me. I almost gagged on the reek of stale cigar smoke and sour alcohol.

"Sluice?" I choked out, reaching forward. I felt a grizzled beard, leathery skin, and bushy eyebrows. I moved my hands down to his chest and felt his overalls, then moved them back up to his face.

"Sluice! It's you! Oh my God!"

Sluice's mouth opened and closed several times, but of course I couldn't hear the words. Maybe it didn't matter, coming from Sluice. Even in broad daylight I might not have understood him anyway.

"Sluice! I can't hear you, remember? I'm deaf. And since I can't see you either, I can't lip-read you. We're going to have to work out some kind of communication system. Do you understand?"

I felt him say something, then nod his head. I could only hope my words were sinking in.

"Good. Listen. When I ask a question, just nod up and down for yes and shake your head for no, okay?"

Sluice nodded against my hand again.

"Great. First of all, are you all right?"

I could feel his mouth moving, then a nod. He took my hand and moved it to the back of his head. It felt wet and matted. Blood.

"You're hurt!"

He returned my hand to his face and shook his head. Although I had felt blood, I had to take him at his word. At least for now.

"Okay, we'll talk about how this happened later. Right now we have to figure out a way to get out of here. Otherwise, it could be days—" decades? I wondered "—before they find us. All right?"

I seemed to be substituting "all rights" for the "GAs"—"Go Aheads" on the TTY. He nodded again. It was a good system. I went ahead.

"Do you have any idea where we are? Which mine shaft this might be?"

Sluice shook his head.

"Me either. Could be anywhere. All right, let me think."

I took my hand from his face and felt along the wall of the shaft. With one hand I explored the entire room, no bigger than a six-by-six-foot cubicle, I guessed. The sides were rough, and my hand quickly grew sore from rubbing over the surface. But it wasn't what I felt on the jagged wall that gave me hope. It was the sensation I had when I pulled my raw hand away.

A slight breeze.

At first I thought it might be Sluice's breath. His exhalations were powerful stuff. But I took in a whiff and found the air to be fresh, almost fragrant. Hopefully that meant we weren't too far from an opening.

In the darkness I had no idea how deep the shaft was. It was time to find out. I felt the ground for some pebbles and brought up a handful. Standing against one wall, I began tossing the pebbles up and slightly forward, to determine some kind of distance.

"Sluice, tap me when you hear the rock hit the ground." I put my hand on his face and felt him nod. I threw a small rock and didn't have to be told when it landed. It had ricocheted against the opposite wall and hit me in the head. "Ouch!"

I would have to be careful dodging rebounds.

I threw a half dozen more pebbles into the air, each one higher—I hoped—than the last. Sluice tapped me each time one landed. It was clear the shaft was deep and we wouldn't be able to just piggyback and climb out.

I continued to inch my way around the shaft, aiming each pebble up and forward, as high as I could throw. I caught a few more on the shoulder and foot. On the eleventh toss, Sluice didn't tap me.

"Sluice? Are you all right?" I put my hand on his face. He nodded.

"You didn't tell me when that last rock landed. I thought I might have got you."

He shook his head and tried to say something—I could feel his jaw moving rapidly.

"I can't hear you, remember? Shall we go on?"

He shook his head forcefully this time.

"What is it? What's wrong?" I asked.

Sluice reached up and took my hand. He turned around, facing away from me, and placed my hand over the back of his own. It felt something like what a blind person might do. Slowly he raised his hand, mine still attached to the back of it, and gestured tossing something up. I had no idea what he was trying to tell me.

Suddenly his hand turned upside down, palm up, and mine followed. He turned around, sliding my hand off his, placed my palm on his shoulder—and lifted it up. A shrug—the universal sign for "I don't know."

"Sluice! Are you saying the pebble never hit the ground?" I cried.

Sluice took my hand and moved it to the side of his face. He nodded vigorously, just like Helen Keller's teacher in *The Miracle Worker*. I got goose bumps.

"The pebble never hit the ground!" I repeated. He nodded again. "That means it must have landed on some kind of surface up there. And that means there should be an opening. We have to try again, to make sure."

I picked up a few more pebbles and tossed them as nearly as I could in the same general direction. Sluice confirmed each throw with a shrugged shoulder I felt through my hand.

"All right, Sluice! It's probably a drift mine—one that tunnels in from the side of the hill, gradually getting lower and lower. Didn't miners dig out a bunch of horizontal escape hatches in case they were trapped? That's got to be it!"

If it was indeed a drift, we had a good chance of crawling out of this death trap—unless, after all these years, it had somehow been blocked along the way. I had no time to think about that now. It was time for a boost.

"Sluice, I need you to help me up so I can climb into that drift. Are you feeling well enough to hold my weight?"

Sluice nodded.

"What about your head?"

He shrugged. We were having a real conversation here.

"Okay, let's give it a try. Where are your hands?" I felt for them and had him clasp them together to make a foothold. I held onto his shoulders and stepped into his laced hands. My foot went right through his fingers, and I nearly lost my balance.

"Are you all right?" I asked.

He nodded and locked his fingers together again, tapping my arm with them, urging me to try once more. I did. This time, under his wobbly support, I stepped up and his hands held. I reached up and felt for the opening of the drift.

Solid rock all the way to my fingertips. I wasn't high enough.

"Sluice, I can't reach the opening. I'm going to try to climb up on your shoulders. Do you think you can hold me?" I felt his head nod against my pant leg. Uh-oh. I was really going to have to do this stunt. Wished I'd taken some circus classes, gymnastics, anything. Too late now. I was about to climb out on a high wire without a net.

I grasped Sluice's furry head, trying not to touch his wound, and used it to balance myself as I lifted a foot onto his shoulder. After taking a few seconds to regain my balance—which isn't that good to begin with—I held on tighter and slid my other foot up and onto the other shoulder. I was probably poking both Sluice's eyes out or pulling his hair in my tight, mostly one-handed grasp, but at that moment I didn't care. All I cared about was not falling.

After a few more seconds and a mental pep talk, I began to straighten out my legs and back, using the shaft wall as support. I could feel Sluice swaying beneath me and wondered how long he could hold out. He was old, wounded, not terribly strong, and possibly still under the influence of alcohol, which didn't make for a sturdy ladder. But what choice did we have?

I kept stretching and straightening, using my fingers on the wall to guide my way. When I stood erect, I let out the breath I'd apparently been holding for the past few moments. I knew I had to hurry—Sluice couldn't last much longer. But every move I made felt like the beginning of a large tumble to the ground. Hurrying would only increase my chances of falling.

Once I'd reached my full height, I started moving my hand up the wall to find the opening. There it was, about a foot above my head. Even though I'd been sure there was an opening, it still felt like a miracle to confirm it.

"It's here, Sluice! I found the drift!"

Sluice patted my foot in response. "All right, now I just have to get myself up and in there. Can you hold on?"

He patted my foot again.

"Here goes." I slung my good arm up and into the hole, right up to the elbow. I could feel myself lift a couple of pounds off Sluice's shoulder, but I didn't have enough leverage to hoist myself completely up and into the tunnel. Especially with one useless arm.

"Sluice, I can't quite get a grip. I need a couple more inches so I can get my chest into the hole and hoist myself the rest of the way."

I felt like crying. We were so close, but I just couldn't make the reach. And there was no way I could hold Sluice on my shoulders. I started to bend my legs to come down when Sluice slapped my foot. I froze.

"What?"

I straightened up and waited a few seconds, wondering why Sluice had slapped me. Then I knew. He was trying to lift up one of my feet—and place it on his head!

"No, Sluice! I'll break your neck!"

But he physically insisted, pushing my foot onto the top of his head and holding it there with a tight grasp.

"Okay, I'll try it, but only for a second, all right?"

He patted my foot again, giving me the go-ahead. I started to put my weight on that foot. With my arm gripping the floor of the drift, I slowly eased myself up, straightening my bent leg and shifting my weight to Sluice's head. I could feel him trembling beneath me.

It was all I needed to get enough leverage to pull myself into that drift. I leaned into the tunnel as far as I could, then dragged myself forward with my good arm, using my legs to push against the mine shaft wall. My feet skidded against the wall, but finally one foot made contact with a jagged edge, and within moments I was inside the drift.

"We did it! Sluice, we did it!"

I couldn't see Sluice, but I thought I could feel his joy and relief. "Now sit tight. I'm going to see if I can follow this drift out of the mine and get help. I think I've got a good chance. I can feel a strong breeze up here, and I smell the evergreens. Are you all right?"

I realized I wouldn't be able to tell in this blackness if Sluice was in trouble. "Sluice! Throw a pebble up here to let me know you're all right."

I waited several minutes in the darkness for a sign from Sluice.

Nothing.

"Sluice? I need to know if you're all right. Throw a rock at me."

I waited several more minutes. Still nothing. My heartbeat began to go into hyperdrive. Something was wrong with Sluice. My efforts to climb into the drift had undoubtedly put him over the edge.

I had to get help.

"Sluice, I'll be right back. I'm going to get help. Just sit tight."

Tight. Hell, I didn't know the meaning of the word until I tried to make my way out of that drift.

☞ CHAPTER XXI.

THE OPENING was spacious compared to the tunnel I would have to crawl through to get out. Claustrophobia swept over me as I squeezed inside the drift. The circumference had to be no larger than a medium pizza, and I was feeling like an extra-large.

Dragging myself through the tunnel took every bit of strength and determination I had, especially with my useless arm, which I suspected was broken. It ached every time I moved it, but I had no choice. I had to keep going. I just prayed that this drift didn't come to a dead end. There was certainly a good chance it went nowhere.

But the breeze was increasing and so was the scent of pine. Nothing had ever smelled so good, not Dan's cologne or a two-pound box of dark chocolates. I don't know how long I was in that tunnel or how much distance I covered in the darkness, but it seemed like forever and it seemed like miles. Just about the time I began to feel a little more breeze against my face and arms, I bumped into something hard with my outstretched hand.

"No!" I screamed.

It was the thing I most dreaded: A dead end. My eyes filled with tears, more at the frustration of coming so far only to have it end like this than at the fear of never getting out of this place.

I composed myself and reached out again to feel the rocky wall blocking my path. I wanted to hit the damn thing with my good arm, but I couldn't get the leverage in my position, lying on my stomach. Good thing. I probably would have broken my other arm, too.

I started to pull back when I realized I could still feel air. Where was it coming from? I moved my hand along the top of the tunnel, checking for a hole, but it was solid. I arched my back and touched the other side of the tunnel. Just at my fingertips I felt the wall give way to nothing.

There was a hole, just off to the left side of my head!

The tunnel had been dug out at a sharp angle, almost ninety degrees, completely changing the direction. If I could just scrunch myself up, I might be able to inch my way around the corner. Once my torso was in the new wing, all I had to do was get my legs around the bend and I could return to propelling my-self forward.

I positioned my legs. But as soon as I pushed off the flat sur-face with my feet, the ground completely gave way underneath me. The tunnel ended abruptly right after the turn, plunging me five or six feet down, into some manzanita bushes full of sharp points.

"Fuck!" I screamed. Didn't care if my mother heard me curse. I just had to let it out. Partly because I was riddled with scrapes, cuts, and prickles. But mostly because I was outside. And free!

I took a moment to collect myself, apologized to my mother for swearing, and achingly pushed myself to standing. The open-ing to the drift had been well covered by overgrowth. I'll bet no one had found this part of the mine in years. Thank goodness I had, from the inside out.

Sluice. I had to get help fast. After orienting myself to the lights of Flat Skunk, I knew I was on Buzzard Hill. I half ran, half slid down the embankment, now deserted in the darkness. The lights kept me focused and on track, and it wasn't long before I reached the road. I flagged down the first car I saw and could only hope it wasn't my attacker.

The car slowed down as I stood waving in the middle of the road. I held my hand over my eyes to shield them from the headlights but couldn't make out anything about the car or its driver, until the vehicle pulled up alongside me. Another ubiquitous SUV. The shadowed figure of the driver leaned out the window and into the dim light.

"Dan!" I said, relief pouring over me. "How did you find me?"

Dan got out of the car and put his arms around me. He looked me over briefly, then held me tight. It hurt to be held, but I didn't care.

"Thank God. I knew something had happened to you when you didn't come back for sex."

I wanted to laugh, but all I could manage was a small grin, and even that was painful.

"We've got to get you to the hospital. You can tell me what happened on the way." He started to lead me to the passenger side of the car, but I held up.

"No, wait! Sluice is still in there. I've got to get the sheriff!"

"In where?" Dan looked up toward the darkened hills.

"In a mine shaft. Somebody—I don't know who—threw us both in there. I managed to crawl out through a drift, but Sluice is still in there. And I think he's badly hurt."

Dan pulled out his cell phone. "All right, look, I'll call an ambulance, have you taken to the hospital, then I'll go get the sheriff—"

"No! We have to get him now. I won't leave until he's safe. Take me to the sheriff." I pulled the car door open and slid in slowly, trying to move as little as possible. If I groaned too much, I was afraid Dan would take me to Emergency, and that would just have to wait. I stifled the pain and said, "Hurry!"

Dan took off like a bat out of a mine shaft, and we were in front of the sheriff's office in minutes. Sheriff Mercer was reclining in his wooden chair, his feet on the desk, eyes covered with his cap. He'd been asleep, but he jumped as we burst through the door.

After he called for assistance from the Whiskey Slide sheriff and a couple of deputies and EMTs, I told him the whole story in detail. When they'd gathered the necessary tools and equipment for rescuing Sluice from the mine shaft, I led them to the opening where I'd escaped, praying Sluice was still alive.

As I recounted my crawl through the drift, we managed to locate the main shaft where Sluice and I had been dumped. It was one of many abandoned links to the old Buzzard Mine, once boarded up, but now exposed. Sheriff Mercer called down into the darkness to Sluice, but I could tell by his expression there was no answer. He shone his flashlight into the ten-foot pit, and I saw the inert body of Sluice, curled into a fetal position at the bottom.

"Hurry!" I cried, but the rescue technicians were already at work. While one of the paramedics was being lowered into the shaft, another prepared medical supplies for Sluice. I watched as the EMT reached Sluice, checked his vitals, and finally called up to his partner. I couldn't lip-read him in the semi-darkness of the shaft, but I knew what the thumbs-up sign meant.

I burst into tears.

I couldn't fight Dan any longer. Once Sluice was out of the pit and on his way in the ambulance, Dan drove me to the hospital where some militant nurses covered me with about four thousand bandages. The bandages didn't even have little cartoon characters on them. I also got a cast from Orthopedics; that was cool. My left arm was indeed broken at the wrist. Dan was the first one to sign the pristine cast. He wrote something naughty using the manual alphabet letters. Unfortunately, one of the militant nurses knew sign language. She wasn't amused.

I stopped by Emergency to check on Sluice but he'd been treated and moved to a semi-private room. Naturally he wasn't allowed visitors at that hour. I'd have to wait until morning to find out what had happened to him. Dan took me home and tucked me in bed, then carefully got in next to me, trying not to touch my bruises, scrapes, gashes, wounds, lesions, abrasions, and other injuries. He said some mushy stuff, but I was too bleary-eyed to read his lips. I think he said something about settling down, making a commitment, stuff like that, but I was fading fast. Maybe he just wanted sex. Life-threatening situations can do that for the libido. If he finally had sex that night, it was in his dreams.

My dreams were nightmares. First, I was trapped in Sluice's trailer, then I was trapped in the mine shaft, then I was trapped in a hospital room with militant nurses, and then I was trapped in a jail cell. The last thing I remember before I woke up screaming was being trapped again. This time in the trunk of a car.

Dan was gone when I awoke late. Probably heard my nightmare screams and didn't want to get involved. Oh well, I had more

important things on my mind. Like figuring out who tried to kill
me. And Sluice. Twice. I had it narrowed down to one suspect
now. And I had a hunch he knew I was onto him because he'd
left an important clue behind in his wake: the plastic bag that
had nearly become my body bag.

Chester Orland.

He'd used the same type of plastic bag to cover the geologist's
body. Apparently, he had a supply of them, left over from his water slide plans that never developed. I TTY'd the sheriff, but
Rebecca intercepted the call—I could tell by her typing.

"SHERIFFS DEPARTMENT HOW CAN I HELP YOU"

When I figured she was done typing, I went ahead. "Hi
Rebecca. Is your boss there? GA"

"IS THIS CONNOR"

Duh. "Yes, Rebecca. Can you put Sheriff Mercer on? GA"

"HES NOT HERE HES OUT ON A CALL IS THERE ANYTHING I
CAN HELP YOU WITH"

"Just tell him to meet me at Chester's place when he comes
in. It's urgent. OK? GA"

"WILL DO HEARD YOU GOT YOURSELF BANGED UP LAST NIGHT
ARE YOU ALL RIGHT"

"I'm fine. A few scratches. A broken wrist. A sore butt. Shall
I go on? GA"

"NO THAT'S FINE IM GETTING A RASH JUST READING YOUR
WORDS YOU TAKE CARE NOW"

I typed "SK" for "Stop Keying," took the receiver off the TTY,
and placed it back on the phone. I'd swing by Dan's office to see if
I could get some backup at Chester's. I needed to get over there
before Chester figured out what I had figured out and destroyed
those bags.

I drove to the office, favoring my good arm, and ran up the
stairs, hoping Dan was in, but of course he wasn't. I thought

about renting the room out since he was never there. I would have spent a few minutes wondering what he was up to, but I didn't have time. I left a sticky note on his door and headed back to my car.

The tourists were crawling all over Buzzard Hill when I got there. They looked like locusts, come to eat up everything in sight. I'd thought they would have abated, but their numbers seemed to have doubled. Only a plague would help us now.

I caught sight of Chester talking with Jana and Tim Joseph, the bogus archeologists. Actually, it looked more like an argument than a chat. Chester was pointing one way and the couple was pointing the other way. Every few seconds one of them stomped a foot.

Perfect timing.

I kept to the bushes as I headed up the hill toward Chester's ranch house. The sprawling house didn't look much like it must have back in the late 1800s. The place had been added onto several times, in a kind of disorganized fashion, much like a patchwork quilt. The original homestead had probably been absorbed completely by the additions—and they all looked as if they'd been built by Chester himself. Uneven boards, a tar paper roof, a rickety porch about to collapse under the weight of Chester's abandoned projects. I spotted a pile of old signs promising various aborted ventures, including the water slide park.

Now to find the plastic bags. If they still existed.

I snooped around the yard looking for places Chester could store stuff and found enough discarded odds and ends to start an antique store—or perhaps a recycling center. Worthless junk, piled in sheds, under cellar doors, in fenced-in areas, some just lying in the backyard, hidden from view of the casual observer.

No plastic bags anywhere.

Under cover of bushes, I ducked around the front of the house and checked to make sure Chester was still yakking it up with the Joseph couple. I had to take a look inside the house, and I didn't want him sneaking up on me. Been there, done that.

He was still pointing and stomping, about twenty yards away. Now was my chance. I headed around the back again and pushed at a half-opened window. It gave. I climbed in, favoring my good arm, which made it a little awkward to move through the small opening. Landing on the floor, I broke my fall with my other hand. That was all I'd need—another broken arm.

I shook off the pain and scanned the room, looking for storage space, a hiding place, or any other area where the bags could be kept. After five minutes of opening cupboards, drawers, bedroom doors, closet doors, and pantry doors, I came upon the door to the basement.

Uh-uh. No way was I going down there. I'd seen too many horror movies to know you didn't go into dark basements in your sexy nightgown when you were alone in the house.

But what the hell. This wasn't a horror movie, the basement had a light, there were people nearby, and I had on jeans and a T-shirt. I figured I was fairly safe.

I headed down the steps, half expecting Jonesy, the cat from *Alien*, to jump out at me, but it never happened. When I reached the bottom step, no one grabbed my ankle. And when I stepped into the basement, the lights didn't suddenly go out.

Instead, I found what I was looking for. A big cardboard box full of black plastic bags large enough to carry rock samples, to slide on a water slide—or to stuff a body into. The box was labeled POLYPROPYLENE TRANSPORT BAGS—HEAVY DUTY. I grabbed one and ran up the stairs, skipping every other step. My heart was racing like a ticking bomb. One more step and I was out of there. I shoved open the door, hitting the obstruction that now stood in my way of escape.

Chester.

With a rifle.

And a really bad attitude.

"What the fuck are you doing in my house?"

☞ CHAPTER XXII.

"CALM DOWN, Chester. This isn't what it looks like." I dropped the bag and held both hands up as if that would keep him from pulling the trigger.

"It looks like you're in my house. Snooping around my stuff."

Okay, that *was* what it looked like. Time to do what I did best. Lie.

"I wasn't snooping…I was on my way up the hill…to see how things were going…and I thought I saw someone going into your house. I tried calling to you…but you were so busy talking to that couple…I just thought I'd check for myself, you know with all the crazy things that have been happening around here—"

"Shut up. You were snooping and now you're lying. I have the right to shoot you as an intruder on my property." He raised the gun. My armpits tingled. He wouldn't—

The sound of a loud blast ripped through deaf ears. My heart and breath stopped. Before I could collapse into a pool of blood, Sheriff Mercer stepped out from behind Chester.

"Hold it right there, Chester." The sheriff held his own rifle on Chester. I looked down at my chest, wondering if this was what it felt like to be shot—just numb. But there was no blood. No wound. Nothing but a rapidly beating heart pounding beneath my T-shirt. I could actually see it.

I looked up. Sheriff Mercer nodded toward the wall behind me. Several feet to the left, there was a big splintered hole where he'd fired the rifle to scare Chester. And he'd done a good job. Chester held his rifle by one hand in the air and had lost all color in his usually ruddy face.

"Don't shoot! I didn't do nothin'. She was in here snooping around, and I was just trying to find out what she was up to. I wasn't gonna shoot her!"

"Put the rifle on the floor, Chester. Now!"

Chester leaned over, set the rifle carefully on the floor, and raised his hands back up. "I'm telling you, Sheriff, I wasn't gonna do nothing."

"Then why did you have the rifle, Chester?"

"'Cause there was an intruder in my house! And with all that's been going on, I wanted to protect myself." He really looked frightened. Probably because he knew he was going to jail for murder.

Sheriff Mercer took Chester out to his patrol car where he handcuffed him and locked him in the back seat. I followed them, carrying the plastic bag I'd dropped when my hands had turned to butter. I thrust it at the sheriff when he was done.

Sheriff Mercer looked at it, then at me. "What's this?"

"A plastic bag."

"I know that."

"Look familiar?"

Sheriff Mercer studied it, then me. He was clueless.

"It's like the plastic bag he stuffed me in when he threw me in that mine shaft!"

The sheriff took it from me and tossed it on the passenger

seat of the patrol car. But his attention seemed to be on something Chester was saying in the backseat. I couldn't make it out from where I was standing.

"What did he say?"

"Nothing. He's just cursing up a storm and calling you a thief, a liar, and a bunch of other things. I'll take care of this, C.W. You took a big risk going into his place. That was stupid, you know."

"I couldn't find you. I told your dispatcher where I was, and I tried to make sure he wouldn't catch me."

"But he did, didn't he? And if I hadn't got that message from Rebecca, you might not be standing here right now."

I shuddered. He was right. It *was* stupid, even though I thought I'd been careful. Still, I'd found what I was looking for. And the Mother Lode Murderer would be going away for a long time.

Mother Lode Murderer. That reminded me, I had a newspaper to run and a headline to write. This case was over, and I had a first-person account of the details. I headed for my office, eager to get the piece done and to press before the *Monitor* or *Bee* got the story. I didn't even check in on Dan in my haste to get to my computer.

But as I sat there pulling together the sequence of events and the details of the deaths, there was still something off about the whole picture.

Gail.

What did poor Gail have to do with Chester and his plan to bilk a bunch of naïve tourists out of their money with those phony gold nuggets and worthless investments?

Then it came to me. The one time all the victims and/or suspects were together was in the diner the night before Gail died. So who, exactly, was there?

Gail—now deceased.

Her husband, Josh, currently in jail for her murder.

Susie, the innocent bystander, now under the auspices of Social Services. I felt another twinge of guilt that I still hadn't been able to rescue her. But I promised myself I would, now that this was all over.

So who else was there?

Sluice, sitting by himself, three sheets to the wind. His life had been in jeopardy twice—once in the fire and once in the mine shaft.

And then the booth with the men. One wearing a USGS cap—Mike Melvin—also murdered.

Another guy, unidentified.

And Chester.

Chester had the most to gain by Sluice's death, if Sluice was the rightful owner of the Buzzard Hill property. If Mike Melvin knew something about all this—if they were in on the bogus gold discovery together—Chester might have killed him to protect himself.

The third guy might also have been a target if he was involved in whatever was going on. In fact, the third guy might even be lying dead in another mine shaft somewhere, as yet undiscovered.

But what about Gail? Why would Chester have been threatened by her?

And then I knew.

It had taken me this long to figure it out because I was deaf. Being deaf is normal for me, so I don't think about hearing much. But Gail was hearing. She'd been signing with her family at the diner so Chester had probably assumed she was deaf, too. The three men probably talked freely, thinking the family couldn't hear anything, and Sluice was too drunk to understand what was going on. But just in case, Chester tried to get rid of Sluice—and his property deed.

When he somehow found out Gail was not deaf—that she had heard everything that they talked about that night—he hit her over the head hard enough to end her life and stuffed her into the car trunk to make it look like Josh had killed his own wife!

I had it all figured out. Except for one thing.

Who was the third man at Chester's table? Tim Joseph, the archeologist? I'd seen him arguing with Chester.

I had to talk to Josh one more time—if the sheriff would let me. Currently I was *persona non grata* at his office.

—⁀•⁀—

Sheriff Mercer had Chester locked up in the cell next to Josh's by the time I arrived. He frowned when he saw me enter, and headed for his desk.

"Sheriff, I have to talk to Josh!" I pleaded as he sat down.

"Sorry, C.W. No can do."

"Sheriff! Please. It's possible Chester may be telling the truth—at least some of it. I think there was a third man involved in all this—whatever it is—and Josh may be able to tell us who it was. *He* may have been the one who killed Gail."

"It's too late—"

"What! You're still mad at me for breaking one of your rules? After all I've done to help you with this case, you're still going to punish me? That's ridiculous!"

"You finished?" he said calmly. His serenity made me feel like a wild woman. Maybe I was.

"No! Not until you let me see Josh!"

He folded his arms over his chest and smirked. I hated that look.

"What?"

"Josh is gone."

I was dumbfounded. You might say deaf-and-dumbfounded.

"What do you mean, he's gone? Is he—" I got a chill thinking about what I was about to say.

"He's alive. He didn't commit suicide or anything like that. He's been taken to Sacramento to await trial."

"Oh, no! But I have to talk with him.... What am I supposed to do now?"

"You could go to Sacramento, but I doubt they'll let you just waltz in and start signing to the prisoner like you do here." Another smirk. The next time I put his face in the paper, I'd add a mustache, bushy eyebrows, and a wart on his nose.

I collapsed in the chair next to the sheriff's desk. What now? Sluice couldn't tell me anything. He was generally incoherent, and now he was in really bad shape physically. Besides, those Nazi nurses probably wouldn't let me near him.

Now Josh was gone. My last chance of finding out who that other guy was. Unless Chester talked. That was unlikely because he knew whoever had been at that diner with him knew too much—whatever that was.

It was hopeless. There wasn't anyone who—

Oh, yes there was!

I ran out of the door so fast, I forgot to close it.

—◆—

I hopped in my car and made the drive to the Social Services office in Whiskey Slide in nearly half the usual time. Luckily, the sheriff of Whiskey Slide had better things to do than sit at the side of the road waiting for me to speed by. She was probably having a latte with Sheriff Mercer.

Social Services was located in the same two-story concrete building as the sheriff's office. The date "1902" was carved in relief across the top of the entry, flanked by a couple of weather-beaten gargoyles. Sheriff Mercer coveted the Whiskey Slide sheriff's office. It had six cells, three rotating dispatchers, and three deputies. This was the big time.

Victoria Serpa's office was on the second floor at the end of a long, dark hallway. It looked like the walls had been painted over more times than Jilda's nails. I entered and found a secretary at her desk, talking on the phone. She held up a finger, signaling me to wait a moment. I didn't have time. I scanned the names on the two inner doors and headed into Victoria Serpa's office.

A curly-haired woman with freckles and rosy cheeks looked up. Her brown hair was highlighted with gold strands and almost formed a halo around her head. I wondered if she were as angelic as she looked. She'd been a tiger the last time I'd had to deal with her.

"Yes?" she said, looking up from her desk. The surface was stacked high with file folders. I half expected it to be wrapped in red tape. "Oh, it's you. What can I do for you, Ms. Westphal?"

I took a seat opposite her so I could read her more easily. "I'm a friend of Josh Littlefield, remember? You have his daughter, Susie, under your protective care."

I expected her to at least nod her head, but she gave me a blank stare. I had probably already breached confidentiality just by saying Susie's name.

"Susie Littlefield," I said. "The little girl you picked up at the bed-and-breakfast in Flat Skunk. I was there." I waited.

"I'm afraid I can't help you," she finally said.

"You don't even know what I want yet!" I leaned forward, frowning.

"I'm afraid you're going to have to leave—"

"Wait just a damn minute! I think Susie is in danger. We've had a couple of murders in Flat Skunk—I'm sure you've read about them. In fact, that's why she's in your custody. I think Susie might know who the real killer is!"

"Her father was arrested—"

"It's not Josh! And she might know who it is!"

"Well, even if it wasn't her father, it's ridiculous to think she could identify someone. She's only a little girl. And she's deaf-and-dumb."

"She's not dumb! And she's not mute! She's—"

"That's not what I meant. It's just a figure of speech."

"It's not a figure of speech. It's a label that perpetrates a negative and false description of deaf people. But that's not the point. The point is, she's in danger!"

"Well, we have her well cared for, I assure you. She's been placed in a good foster home until other arrangements can be made. Now, please, let us handle the protection of Susie. That's our job."

"But—"

Victoria Serpa pressed a button on her phone and said something I couldn't make out. In seconds the secretary appeared at the door.

"Courtney will escort you out, Ms. Westphal. That is, either she will, or someone from the sheriff's office will. It's your choice."

I started to say something, then gave up. This was hopeless. I had dealt with the bureaucracy of Social Services before, and it was nearly impossible to get them to break a single rule. Writing a grant proposal for world peace would have been simpler.

I got up and left the office without another word.

But not before I had managed to jam my wadded-up business card in the lock.

I learned that trick from Nancy Drew.

☞ CHAPTER XXIII.

IT WAS ALMOST noon. Time for lunch. I headed for my car and waited until I saw the two women, accompanied by a third I didn't recognize, heading out of the building. I figured I'd have at least thirty minutes to find the file that contained the name of Susie's foster parents—if the old wadded-card-in-the-lock worked. And the neighboring sheriff's deputies didn't catch me breaking and entering. And I didn't set off any alarms.

I stopped myself from thinking of all the possibilities for failure. I was an optimist. This was going to work.

I made my way up the stairs to the second floor, avoiding the elevator to keep from being spotted. The stairwell was deserted. I opened the door to the second floor hallway and peered in. No one but us ghosts. I headed down the hall.

The door to the office was locked, as I expected. I pushed it, and it swung open easily. Thanks, Nancy, I thought. Now can you help me find the file I need?

She didn't answer, so I headed for the inner office of Victoria Serpa and *The Secret of the Mysterious Filing Cabinet*. I yanked open the first drawer, searching for Susie by her last name,

Littlefield. The names in the drawer ended with "Jackson." Anyone I knew? I wondered. None of my business. Things were complicated enough. I closed the drawer and moved to the middle one.

The files glided out, all neatly arranged from "K" to "O." I thumbed through the "L"s and found "Little" and "Livorna." No Littlefield.

"Shit!" I may have said aloud, and slammed the drawer shut, then remembered I was covert and that other people could hear the noise, even if I couldn't. I made myself a promise to curb my frustration and be more careful with my vocalizations.

I had another thought. Gail had kept her last name. Maybe Susie was under Gail's name. What was it? Parker. Peters. Peck. Peter Piper…Pike! That was it.

I tried the third drawer, letters "P" through "Z," but there was nothing under "Pike." Damn! I didn't have time to go through every name in her filing cabinet in case it had been misplaced. Not that this anal-retentive social worker would misplace anything.

I turned to go, then glanced at the desk piled high with files. "Please, Nancy," I whispered as I began digging through the orderly stack. About halfway through I found it: "Littlefield, Susie, #8377089." Flipping open the cover, I found the name of the foster parents. "Swec, Barbara and Leonard." I only copied down the address on Placer Place—the phone number was useless to me—and returned the file to where I'd found it in the pile.

Then, like *The Ghost of Blackwood Hall*, I disappeared as fast as I could.

—◆—

I sort of knew where Placer Place was. A development of new homes had recently gone up on the other side of the highway, about halfway between Whiskey Slide and Flat Skunk. Retirees and young couples who couldn't afford the Bay Area prices were streaming into the Mother Lode, demanding golf courses, Home Depots, and Starbucks. They were the real gold diggers. They'd strip the land of its natural beauty, cause overcrowding, heavier traffic, and more stoplights, and change this historic frontier forever. I hated the thought.

But I'd try not to hold that against the Swec family, Barbara and Leonard. After all, they were caring for little Susie. They must be good people, in spite of wanting to rape and pillage my land.

I drove up the pristine street, presently landscaped with pavement and dirt. Soon the community would be filled with bougainvillea from the South, flowers from back East, and trees I thought only grew in Hawaii.

The Swec house at least managed to put up a play structure in their dirt. I figured the Swecs hadn't bought it just for little Susie, so they must have other children. In fact, two little girls were climbing on the colorful plastic structure as I drove up. I parked the Chevy and got out, hoping Susie would remember me—or at least not panic and run screaming into the house signing, "Help! Stranger!"

While the other little girl continued to practice her climbing skills, Susie noticed me immediately and stood at the foot of the plastic ladder, staring at me. I began signing as I crossed the street.

"Hi, Susie! Remember me?" I signed slowly, with a big smile, hoping I looked nonthreatening at the very least, benevolent at best.

She didn't reply but her eyes were locked on mine. She tucked her chin down and pushed one shoulder forward—body language for self-protection.

"I'm a friend of your dad," I continued, moving closer with each sign. "We had dinner together, remember, at the restaurant with the big murals on the wall? You colored a picture for me. A horse."

She nodded slightly, then signed, "Silver Star."

I nodded my head and my hand simultaneously. "Yes, that's the name of your favorite horse, right? Silver Star."

She looked at me, frowning, then signed, "Where's my daddy?"

I didn't know what to say. I couldn't tell her he was in jail for allegedly killing her mother. While I didn't mind lying to strangers, I didn't like lying to kids. I felt bad when I signed, "He'll be here to get you soon."

Tears appeared in Susie's eyes, but she blinked them away. I moved closer. Suddenly she ran forward and threw her arms around me. At that moment I must have been the next best thing to her father. It felt strangely wonderful.

I held her for several minutes, not noticing that the other little girl had disappeared. Moments later a woman appeared at the door, whom I took for Barbara Swec, the foster mother. She was saying something I couldn't make out, but her facial expression was clear. I was trespassing.

I stood up, pulling myself from Susie, but continued to hold her hand.

"Hi," I said aloud. "I'm Connor Westphal. I'm a friend of Susie's. I just wanted to see if she was all right."

Barbara took a step forward. "I said, get away from her, or I'll call the sheriff." A baseball bat dangled from one hand. What had made this woman feel so threatened, I wondered. With that weapon in her hand, I didn't want to argue.

"All right, I'm going. I just wanted to check on her. Let me say good-bye so she won't think I'm abandoning her, too."

Barbara tightened her grip on the bat. "Make it fast. Then get on out of here. I mean it."

I knelt down and began signing. "Susie, does that woman know sign language?"

Susie snapped two fingers onto her thumb, the sign for "No."

"Good. I need your help. When you were in the café with your parents for dessert the other night, there were three men sitting in a booth. Do you remember what they looked like?"

Susie frowned, then held up four fingers.

"Four men?" I asked.

She nodded. "One alone."

"Yes!" I nodded enthusiastically. "And there were three men sitting together. One was big and wore overalls; one had a cap on with letters on it."

Susie nodded.

"Did you see the other man? Can you describe him?"

She frowned, then suddenly darted away, headed for her foster mother at the door. She zipped past her and ducked inside the house. I stood, puzzled. Had I said something to frighten her?

The woman began to step back into the house, still holding the bat at her side. Just as she was about to close the door, Susie slipped past her and ran back to me with a sheet of paper and a black marker in her hand.

As she bent down on the pavement to draw a picture on the paper, I looked up at Barbara. She was lifting the bat.

"Susie said she wants me to bring a picture to her dad," I lied, in the way of an explanation.

"Susie, I have to go," I said to her aloud, knowing she wouldn't hear me. I said it to pacify Barbara and give Susie more time to complete whatever it was she was trying to draw.

I knelt down and watched as she sketched a picture of the Nugget Café booth and the three men. One wore overalls and one wore a cap, just as I had described. She even put the letters "US" on the cap. She was working on the third man, who was wearing a plaid or checked shirt, like every other man in town. Cowboy boots, as common as tobacco spit around these parts. And a third eye.

I frowned at Susie when she looked up, smiling with pride at her drawing. "He had three eyes?" I asked. It looked as if little Susie had a big imagination. She thrust the picture at me just as Barbara came over and pulled her toward the front door.

I held the picture, gave Susie a weak smile, and signed, "Don't worry. You'll be with your dad soon."

She teared up again, as Barbara dragged her into the house and slammed the door.

I stood there, staring at the picture. A third eye. Some kind of monster? Someone who was deformed in some way? Someone wearing a miner's light?

I got in my car and took one more look at the picture before starting the ignition.

Someone wearing a jeweler's loupe?

Oh my God.

—◆—

The assay office was dead, so to speak, when I arrived. A drawing by a little deaf kid wasn't going to cut it with the sheriff, so I thought I'd see if I could find some other connection to Phil Meredith first. Like a smoking murder weapon of some sort.

"Phil?" I called out after giving the bell a chance to alert him of my presence. When he didn't appear within a few minutes, I moved behind the counter to peek into the back room. The place was empty. Odd, since he rarely left the office, but I wasn't about to question my luck. I'd make a quick search and get the hell out of there as fast as I could. I only hoped I could find something significant. It was like looking for a new vein in an old gold mine.

I scanned the back, figuring if he was hiding something, it would most likely be here, away from prying eyes—most prying eyes, anyway. I found a lot of dust, a lot of messy files, and a lot of gold-digging equipment—an ax, a pick, a knife, a shovel. Almost anything in this room would make an effective weapon.

But there was nothing I could see to link Phil Meredith to Gail—or any of the other events, for that matter. I scanned the room again. Maybe there was something in the files. I pulled open a drawer, but Phil's filing system, unlike the social worker's, was chaos. Maybe he could figure it out, but I couldn't make head or tail of it. I slammed the drawer shut and seconds later felt an echo reverberate through the wooden floorboards.

The echo wasn't caused by the file drawer.

I whirled around to see Phil standing in front of the closed door to his back room. His slamming of the door must have caused the vibration beneath my feet. In his arms he held all the evidence I would need to prove he was connected to Gail's murder.

Little Susie.

☞ CHAPTER XXIV.

"LET HER GO!" I screamed.

Susie lay limp in Phil Meredith's arms, not struggling. I couldn't even tell if she was breathing until she opened her eyes and looked at me in terror. At least she was alive.

She had a red welt on one cheek, but no other signs of injury that I could see. Still, I wanted to kill him for what he'd done. I looked around for one of those potential weapons, and suddenly they all seemed miles out of reach. The best I could do was stall him until I could figure out what action to take.

"How did you find her?" I asked, hoping to distract him while I came up with an idea.

Phil Meredith gave me the first smile I'd ever seen on his face. His grin gave me chills. "Easy. I followed you."

"But how did you—"

He cut me off. "Simple as tracking a skunk on a windy day."

"What do you want with Susie? She didn't do anything. I'm the one you want. Let her go!" I moved an inch toward the table, hoping he wouldn't notice.

"I want both of you. I need her, too, so I can make it look like you killed her instead of me."

"You can't be serious! You can't kill her. She's done nothing." I hoped Susie couldn't read my lips, but I'm sure she knew something really bad was going on because she remained limp in Phil's arms. Only her eyes showed any reaction to the situation—they were as wide as a cat's in a dark room. She was terrified, and I didn't blame her. So was I.

"She knows about me," Phil snarled. "And she's the last of them to connect me to anything. Besides you, of course."

"She's only a child! And she's deaf. She won't say anything. She has no idea what it is you've done."

"But if the sheriff gets to talking with her, she just might draw him the same picture she drew you."

Phil had seen the picture! Had he been that close to us at the Swecs' house? How could I not have spotted him? Easily, really. I was too wrapped up in trying to see Susie. And of course I couldn't hear him behind me.

"What about the foster mother, Barbara Swec? Did you kill her, too?"

He shook his head and grinned again. His teeth were mottled, probably from years of chewing tobacco, drinking coffee, and not flossing.

"Then she's going to know you kidnapped Susie."

"Not really. In fact, she's gonna think you did it. You were the last one to see the girl, remember? At least, that's the way she'll tell it to the sheriff. She never saw me sneak in the house and snatch the kid."

God, he was fearless. Damn, what was his plan? I had to think. This guy was smart—he had thought everything out. And when something went wrong, he dealt with it lethally. Now he had plans for Susie and me. I had to keep him distracted until I could grab some kind of heavy or sharp tool off the table.

I took a step closer. Phil reacted instantly by grabbing Susie around her neck with one hand. "Don't even think about it," he said. Susie's eyes blazed with fear.

He was watching me more closely than I thought. Shit! What now? The one he wasn't really watching was Susie.

And that gave me an idea. The only thing I had going for me was the ability to communicate with Susie without Phil knowing. In Sign.

Juiced by adrenaline with this new plan, I bombarded Phil with questions, hoping he was egomaniacal enough to want to answer them. Criminals always thought they were smarter than other people—and they liked to brag about it. Maybe his fat head would be his downfall.

I asked him about his scheme with Chester and he opened up. Told me all about the plan to salt the area around the mine, then sell investments in the worthless land. Before anyone got wise, they'd split the money, spend it on whatever, and tell the investors the gold was gone. But then he got greedy and decided he wanted all the investment money. He killed Mike Melvin, then planned to make it look like Chester had done it. With Melvin dead and Chester in prison, he was the only one left to spend the money.

"But why try to kill Sluice? Why burn his house down and then throw him into that shaft? He would never have understood your plan."

"You don't know that. Sluice is a lot smarter than he acts. I could tell by his eyes he knew something was up. I had no choice but to get rid of him."

"And me?"

"Ain't it obvious? You were getting too close."

While he blabbered on, I began to sign slowly to Susie. Immediately I could see in her frightened eyes that she was following my words. Like most deaf people, Susie was highly visual and primed for sign language, even when the signs were subtle. Deaf people can "whisper" in Sign simply by minimizing their hand movements and signing away from another person's peripheral vision.

"See desk?" I whispered in Sign, moving two fingers slightly forward from the side of my leg, then turning my palm down. Susie glanced at the tabletop near Phil, covered with more assaying and mining tools. She nodded her fist with a tiny movement of the wrist.

"See rock?" I signed, my index finger jutting forward an inch. She spotted it and nodded her hand once again.

"Grab and throw." I gestured the action slightly, hoping she understood. All she had to do was cause a distraction that would throw Phil Meredith off balance. Then I'd have a chance to hit him with one of the tools on the counter. Susie was a smart girl, but signing with one hand down at my side may have left some of the meaning a little ambiguous.

"But why did you kill Gail? She wouldn't have figured out your plan," I said to Phil aloud, hoping Susie would take the opportunity to grab one of the many rocks and throw it while Phil was distracted by my questions.

She didn't move.

"I had to kill her 'cause she overheard everything we was talking about at the café. At first I thought she was deaf-and-dumb, but after her husband and kid left, I noticed she was watching us. Then Mama Cody came out from the kitchen and the woman started talking to Mama. That's when I realized she could hear—and probably heard everything we'd said."

I glanced at Susie. Her eyes had moved from me, but her little hand had slowly fallen to her side, closer to the table. She was smarter than I thought, taking her time like that.

I signed, "Now!" and her limp body suddenly sprang to life.

She lunged toward the table, grabbed a good-sized rock and threw it with all her might, thrashing and screaming all the while.

Stunned at the wild child in his arms, Phil's reflexes jerked him into action. He let her go and she tumbled to the floor. Within seconds she'd recovered and had run to me. I pushed her behind my back.

With Phil momentarily distracted, I started throwing every tool and instrument I could find on the nearby work table, bombarding him with steel, iron, wood, whatever. When I ran out of tools, I picked up a tray of what looked like fist-sized chunks of iron pyrite and tossed them at him, one after another, like a baseball pitcher gone mad. I kept stuff flying so fast, all he could do was duck and defend himself from the bombardment with his arms.

The moment I ran out of weapons, Susie and I made a run for it. Phil jumped up, holding the knife, and tried to grab Susie. He snagged her T-shirt with a bloody hand, but she bit him and he let go with what looked like a shriek of pain. As I followed Susie's escape out the door, I slugged Phil with my cast right across the face. I didn't look back to see if he had any teeth left.

We made it outside just as Sheriff Mercer was cruising by in his patrol car, Dan at his side. I had a feeling they'd been looking for us. I screamed for them, and the sheriff halted his car. But before I could tell them what happened, Phil Meredith appeared at the doorway, his face bloodied by my bashing arm.

He held a rifle in his bleeding hands.

Sheriff Mercer pushed open the backseat door of his squad car and waved us in. He jumped out of his seat with his revolver drawn and crouched behind the car door as Dan pulled Susie inside. I fell in behind her, slammed the door behind us, and ducked down behind the front seat.

PENNY WARNER

"What's happening?" I said to Dan, who was bent over in his
seat. He peeked over the top so I could read his lips, keeping his
eyes on the sheriff and Phil.

"Sheriff Mercer is telling Phil to put his gun down...saying,
'It's all over...turn yourself in'..."

Dan stopped talking.

"What? What's happening?" I demanded. I started to lift my
head to see, but Dan shoved me back down again.

"He's inside."

"Who, Phil?"

"Yeah, he went back in the office and closed the door."

"What's Sheriff Mercer doing? He's not going in after him, is
he? That would be suicide."

"The sheriff's on the phone, probably calling for backup, still
covering the door with his gun. Wait. Oh, shit. I think he's going
in after him."

"Oh my God. There's no telling what Phil—"

Dan's eyes widened. He pushed my head down again, and I
reflexively pushed Susie's head down. I waited a minute, then
looked up at Dan. His mouth was open as wide as his eyes.

"What happened? I think I heard something."

"You heard a gunshot."

"Oh, God! What happened? Is it Sheriff Mercer?"

Dan paused, then shook his head. "I don't know. It came
from inside the office."

☞ CHAPTER XXV.

SECONDS LATER the door reopened.

My heart stopped as I peeked up from behind the safety of the seat.

Sheriff Mercer stepped out, his gun at his side. He looked shaken.

"Call an ambulance. Phil Meredith is dead. He shot himself in the head."

———◆———

Susie and I rode together to Mother Lode Memorial Hospital in one ambulance; Phil Meredith rode in another. The sheriff stayed behind with the crime scene and his deputy. Dan notified Social Services of Susie's whereabouts, and then met us at the hospital. Victoria Serpa and Barbara Swec arrived together and retrieved Susie after she was checked and released by the emergency room doctor. All she had was the faintest mark on her face from when Phil had slapped her. I was given a few minutes alone with Susie before she left and promised her that she'd be seeing her daddy very soon. This time I wasn't lying.

The hospital was beginning to feel like my second home. I had to have my cast removed and replaced. I'd damaged it when I'd slugged Phil Meredith's hard head on my way out the door. The emergency room doctor wrapped my arm with a couple of extra layers, in case I had to slug any other killers in the next few weeks.

Sheriff Mercer called Sacramento to let them know the charges against Josh were going to be dropped. I made him promise Josh would hear the news from an interpreter so there wouldn't be any confusion on his part. They owed him that. I wondered what he'd do about the cochlear implant, now that Gail was gone. But we could talk about that later.

Before I let Dan take me home from the hospital, I made him come with me for one last stop. I had to get special permission from the doctor on duty, but when I finished explaining everything that had happened, he just looked at me in disbelief and gave me carte blanche.

I let myself in the room that was clearly marked NO VISITORS. Dan waited in the hall to keep the Nazi nurse at bay. Sluice was watching some reality show on TV, which seemed strange under the circumstances. Hadn't he had enough reality for a while?

"Hi Sluice," I said, trying to distract him from what looked like a half-naked man lying in a pit covered with snakes.

He surprised me by switching off the TV and taking my hand. I gave it a squeeze and smiled, then Sluice released his grip and reached under the sheet. He pulled out a piece of paper.

"The deed!" I said, taking it from his shaky hand. "I thought it was stolen. How did you get it back?"

Sluice mumbled something I couldn't make out. I didn't press it, but I figured he must have stolen it back from Chester—or whoever took it. The old guy was full of surprises—that was half his "charm."

"Dan said to take this directly to Public Records in Sacramento when you're out of here. You and me, together, okay?"

Sluice nodded and slipped the paper back under the sheet. No telling where he was keeping it under there. Didn't want to know. I said good night and slipped out the door as he turned the TV back on. I caught a glimpse of potato bugs—those ugly insects the size of small cars—crawling over someone's face. One of those reality shows. I almost needed the emesis basin.

"Thanks for waiting," I said to Dan as we headed out of the hospital toward his truck. He wrapped an arm around me, and it felt great, in spite of my aches and pains.

"I'll wait as long as it takes," I thought he said.

"What?"

"You heard me."

"No, I didn't. I'm deaf, remember?"

"Only when it suits you."

I wanted to punch him, but with my arm in that cast, I worried I might deal him a lethal blow.

Casper was so happy to see me he almost peed on the floor. I felt the same way but held onto my bladder out of respect for what was left of my dignity. Dan made me a mocha while I played with Casper, then joined me on the floor with two mugs and a bowl of water for my dog. What a guy.

"So, Sluice will probably get his land since Chester will be relocating to the state prison for fraud. Josh will be released any minute now and Susie will get her father back. The sheriff will get his face in the *Eureka!* as a local hero. And you'll get a headline."

"Yep. Although I think I prefer writing about rummage sales and lost cats. I don't need no more stinking headlines."

Dan nodded, but he looked pensive, as if he weren't really listening to me. Wouldn't be the first time.

"What?" I said.

"Nothing."

"What?"

He shrugged, set down his mocha, and took my good hand. With his other hand, he reached into his jeans pocket. "I was just thinking, maybe you and I…you know, maybe we should—"

He pulled out a tiny velvet box.

My mouth dropped open. I felt my skin break into millions of tiny bumps—probably hives. My stomach whirled like a Cuisinart. I couldn't feel my feet.

"So that's what you've been up to!" I gasped, thinking back to his recent disappearances, his evasiveness, his locked desk drawer. He'd been out…shopping.

"Are you all right?" Dan asked, pulling back.

"Yeah, sure, I'm fine. Why?"

"You look…pale. As if you've seen a ghost."

"No, no, I'm fine. I—"

He put the box in my sweaty palm. My fingers wouldn't bend. I felt like I had rigor mortis.

"Connor Westphal—you're scared!"

"No, I'm not! How can you say that? After what I've been through!"

"Oh, no, you're not afraid of trouble. In fact, you welcome it. And you're not afraid of dark mine shafts. Or creepy basements. Or mad killers. But you're afraid of what's in that little box—and what I was about to say."

"I…I… No, I'm not."

"Really?"

"Really!"

"Then open the box."

"I will! I am…" I looked down at the box. Oh my God. I *was* afraid to open it. Where had that come from? Was it fear of losing my independence, after I'd worked so hard to gain it? Fear of commitment after my last boyfriend cheated on me? I looked back up at Dan.

"So what was it you were going to say, anyway?" I braced myself.

"You're stalling."

"I'm not!"

"You sure you're not going to faint or throw up or anything?"

"Of course not. Unless there's a potato bug in the box…" I was rambling. Or stalling. "What?"

"I was going to say, shall we get that legal piece of paper?"

"What, a property deed?"

He reached over and opened the lid of the box.

I looked at the polished gold nugget atop the gold band and smiled. Tears came to my eyes. I couldn't speak.

Silence is golden.

—◆—

Rebecca Warner

About the Author

Penny Warner is the author of over forty books for adults and children, including six in the Connor Westphal mystery series. *Dead Body Language* was nominated for an Agatha Award and won a Macavity for Best First Mystery. Her book for juvenile readers, *The Mystery of the Haunted Caves*, won an Agatha and an Anthony.

The holder of a master's degree in Special Education, Warner teaches child development and sign language at local colleges. She is the author of *Learn To Sign the Fun Way*. She also teaches writing, and with her husband, Tom, she writes and produces mystery fund-raisers for libraries and other organizations. The Warners have two grown children and live in Northern California.

Visit and e-mail Penny Warner on-line at www.pennywarner.com

MORE MYSTERIES
💀 FROM PERSEVERANCE PRESS 💀
For the New Golden Age

Available now—

The Beastly Bloodline, A Delilah Doolittle Pet Detective Mystery
by Patricia Guiver
ISBN 1-880284-69-3
Wild horses ordinarily couldn't drag British expatriate Delilah to a dude ranch. But
when a wealthy client asks her to solve the mysterious death of a valuable show horse,
she runs into some rude dudes trying to cut her out of the herd—and finds herself on a
trail ride to murder.

Death, Bones, and Stately Homes, A Tori Miracle Pennsylvania Dutch Mystery
by Valerie S. Malmont
ISBN 1-880284-65-0
Finding a tuxedo-clad skeleton, Tori Miracle fears it could halt Lickin Creek's annual
house tour. While dealing with disappearing and reappearing bodies, a stalker, and an
escaped convict, Tori unravels the secrets of the Bride's House and Morgan Manor,
which the townsfolk wish to hide.

Slippery Slopes and Other Deadly Things, A Carrie Carlin Biofeedback Mystery
by Nancy Tesler
ISBN 1-880284-64-2
Biofeedback practitioner/single mom/amateur sleuth Carrie Carlin is up to her neck in
snow, sex, and strangulation when her stress management convention is interrupted by
murder on the slopes of a Vermont ski resort.

REFERENCE/MYSTERY WRITING
How To Write Killer Fiction: The Funhouse of Mystery & the Roller Coaster of
Suspense
by Carolyn Wheat
ISBN 1-880284-62-6
The highly regarded author of the Cass Jameson legal mysteries explains the difference
between mysteries (the art of the whodunit) and novels of suspense (the hero's journey)
and offers tips and inspiration for writing in either genre. Wheat shows how to make
your book work, from the first word to the final revision.

Another Fine Mess, A Bridget Montrose Mystery
by Lora Roberts
ISBN 1-880284-54-5
Bridget Montrose wrote a surprise bestseller, but now her publisher wants another one.
A writers' retreat seems the perfect opportunity to work in the rarefied company of
other authors...except that one of them has a different ending in mind.

Flash Point, A Susan Kim Delancey Mystery
by Nancy Baker Jacobs
ISBN 1-880284-56-1
A serial arsonist is killing young mothers in the Bay Area. Now Susan Kim Delancey,
California's newly appointed chief arson investigator, is in a race against time to catch
the murderer and find the dead women's missing babies—before more lives end in flames.

Open Season on Lawyers, A Novel of Suspense
by Taffy Cannon ISBN 1-880284-51-0

Too Dead To Swing, A Katy Green Mystery
by Hal Glatzer ISBN 1-880284-53-7

The Tumbleweed Murders, A Claire Sharples Botanical Mystery
by Rebecca Rothenberg, completed by Taffy Cannon ISBN 1-880284-43-X

Keepers, A Port Silva Mystery
by Janet LaPierre ISBN 1-880284-44-8
Shamus Award nominee, *Best Paperback Original 2001*

Blind Side, A Connor Westphal Mystery
by Penny Warner ISBN 1-880284-42-1

The Kidnapping of Rosie Dawn, A Joe Barley Mystery
by Eric Wright ISBN 1-880284-40-5
Barry Award, *Best Paperback Original 2000.* Edgar, Ellis, and Anthony Award nominee

Guns and Roses, An Irish Eyes Travel Mystery
by Taffy Cannon ISBN 1-880284-34-0
Agatha and Macavity Award nominee, *Best Novel 2000*

Royal Flush, A Jake Samson & Rosie Vicente Mystery
by Shelley Singer ISBN 1-880284-33-2

Baby Mine, A Port Silva Mystery
by Janet LaPierre ISBN 1-880284-32-4

Forthcoming—

A Fugue in Hell's Kitchen, A Katy Green Mystery
by Hal Glatzer
In New York City in 1939, musician Katy Green's hunt for a stolen music manuscript
turns into a fugue of mayhem, madness, and death. Prequel to *Too Dead To Swing.*

The Affair of the Incognito Tenant, A Mystery with Sherlock Holmes
by Lora Roberts
In 1903 in a Sussex village, a young, widowed housekeeper welcomes the mysterious
Mr. Sigerson to the manor house in her charge—and unknowingly opens the door to
theft, bloody terror, and murder.

**Available from your local bookstore or from
Perseverance Press/John Daniel & Co. at (800) 662-8351
or www.danielpublishing.com/perseverance.**